# CREEP AROUND THE CORNER

# CREEP AROUND THE CORNER

*A Spy Novel*

DOUGLAS ATWILL

SANTA FE

Sunstone books may be purchased for educational, business, or sales promotional
use. For information please write: Special Markets Department, Sunstone Press,
P.O. Box 2321, Santa Fe, New Mexico 87504-2321.

Book design • Vicki Ahl
Body typeface • Book Antiqua
Printed on acid free paper

Library of Congress Cataloging-in-Publication Data

Atwill, Douglas.
Creep around the corner : a spy novel / Douglas Atwill.
    p. cm.
ISBN 978-0-86534-654-3 (pbk. : alk. paper)
1. Cold War--Fiction. 2. Europe--Politics and government--1945---Fiction. I. Title.
PS3601.T85C74 2010
813'.6--dc22

                    2009051829

**WWW.SUNSTONEPRESS.COM**
SUNSTONE PRESS / POST OFFICE BOX 2321 / SANTA FE, NM 87504-2321 /USA
(505) 988-4418 / ORDERS ONLY (800) 243-5644 / FAX (505) 988-1025

I WISH TO ACKNOWLEDGE
and thank the following for their help with the manuscript—
Douglas Bland, Walter Cooper, Billy Halsted, John Strand,
Melinda K. Hall, Shelley McGehee, and Sylvia Debenport,
who each read parts of this story or listened patiently
while I read them aloud. If names,
places or incidents seem familiar, they are not.
All of this book is fiction, cooked up from everyday ingredients.

# FAT SCOTTISH PEAS

It furthers one to undertake something.
It furthers one to cross the great water.
— *I Ching*

AS THE MINUTES TO DEPARTURE closed in, Henry Zilbert turned to me and asked, "Are you scared?"

"I'm angry that I got caught."

"Are they still shooting at us in Korea?"

"I don't think so."

"You'll be okay. You're a good shot when you try. Problem is, you don't try very often."

This was the day in May that I was called up by the Middleton draft board. The West Texas summer had come in early and we were waiting in front of the bus station in Henry's convertible, top up and windows open. He looked straight ahead, his way of not showing much emotion or vulnerability. I always admired Henry's lanky posture, good looks, black hair with umber-brown eyes, and wished away my light hair, blue eyes and long-waisted sturdiness.

We had planned to share the Zilbert house on Water Street, Henry's now that his grandfather had died. I would fix up the attic for a studio, starting the first paintings of an art career and Henry could manage the Martin County ranch from the offices on the ground floor. A Dallas architect designed the house in the palmy spring of 1929, but it was not completed until well into the Depression. A shingle-sided, three story mansion with a full basement, it had the only built-in vacuum machine in Middleton, now barely able to suck up the dead flies that piled up beside the painted shut windows.

This would be after we both graduated from university next year. We would open up the windows and give beer parties for all of young Middleton. Before now, there had been plenty of girl friends because Henry was handsome and I was too, I guess, but nothing ever took. The girls went on to the men who really wanted them. Life was good when I was with Henry but now it was ending, or at least being put on hold. Because I had willfully allowed myself to be taken up in the draft, we left my mother in tears an hour earlier. My father could not even mention my name without choking. I had mocked their many years of college support, mother said, and danced away my future with drink and song. Mother had a way with invective.

I said, "The bus is here and there's Mrs. Flack with my papers."

"Who's Mrs. Flack?"

"She is the draft board. You haven't had to deal with her, thanks to your asthma. She told me, *Well, Mr. Coward College Deferral…when the mighty fall.*"

"She looks harmless."

"Not so. I'll miss you, bud." I put my hand on his shoulder and shook his hand. He did not get out of the convertible, but just sat to watch me go. I waved back at him and he tilted his chin upwards, ever so little. Mrs. Flack stood at attention in her flowered house-dress and gave me a pink-gummed smile, like a happy horse, as she handed over my papers and the bus ticket to Arkansas. Have a good two years, Bradford, she said and snorted out another smile.

Basic training in Camp Chaffee was a summer-long blur of chiggers, thunderstorms, disgrace, aches and pain. If I was average in push-ups, chin-ups, sit-ups, squats and running uphill with a forty-pound pack, I earned the top Sharpshooter's Badge, as Henry predicted.

The army had failed that summer to meet its quota with volunteers for the Counterintelligence School in Baltimore, so I, along with two others, was assigned there. We were very lucky young men, they said. Ordinary draftees were rarely accepted. No one thought to check back with Mrs. Flack about my cowardice, however, and how the fallen mighty might be rising once again .

At Baltimore we learned the tricks to becoming a spy, sixteen weeks of them. Ju-jitsu, bridge explosives, sub-machine guns, deadly force, listening devices, poison gas in a fountain pen and surveillance by the book. We drove into the Maryland countryside to shoot a sub-machine gun at cut-out images of the enemy that popped up as we walked along, Russian agents in trench-coats and Chinese fanatics in high collars. I scored a hundred on that, all the painted villains flat in the weeds, the spy-to-be Bradford the envy of his classmates.

However, the instructor told us that we were mere analysts, draftees never able to become full-blown field agents. He made it clear that we were the lowest echelon, the untouchables of espionage, cleaning the safe-house toilets and shining the bullet-proof windows.

That summer, the spoiled boy Bradford, like many before him, lost some of his callowness and became a cog in the machine of war. If not the bravest or the strongest, I was a trained soldier, dagger at the ready. At the graduation ceremony, I felt I was becoming the man, muscles rippling, the superficial student morphed into a trained killer. I practiced my sharp look and angled my khaki cloth cap just so.

After that late November commencement day, two of us waited for a military flight to Labrador, connecting with a six-propellered flight across the ocean to Greenland, and thence to a Scotland refueling, where there was time for a meal at the transient's mess. It was a spread of rump roast, crisp browned potatoes, and fat Scottish peas, served by a red-cheeked, red-haired woman with a soiled apron. She spoke a foreign language that sounded somewhat like English.

A few hours later, we landed at the misty airport at Frankfurt-am-Main and boarded a German train down to Stuttgart, where it was even mistier. It was mid-afternoon and completely dark.

Eric Follum was my traveling companion, a tall Wisconsin farm lad with an elegant nose, pale-blue eyes. So deep was his depression about leaving the States that he had not said more than thirty words the entire trip. I was in no mood to pull him out, engage conversation, the way I was taught. Nice people look after each other, Grandmother Bradford often said, but I had the feeling that family rules for a good life were not operational in the West Germany of 1956.

After I mentioned the early darkness to our driver from the train station to Intelligence Headquarters, he said wait until you see how nasty a German winter can be. As we drove up the hill, Schloss Issel loomed in the fog with dormant rows of grape vines on either side; the yellow-lighted windows shone like curious, unfriendly eyes. Where were the Bronte sisters when I needed them?

Sergeant Major Tetley of the Quarters Detachment waited for us. He said, gruffly but not without sympathy, "Mess is closed up for the night. Bradford, there's an empty bed in room three eighteen. Follum, three twenty-two. Morning formation is o-eight-hundred, so have breakfast early. Corporal Murgon will catch you up to speed tomorrow."

Glancing down further on his clipboard, he said. "We have both of you assigned to Historical Section. Sorry, men." I should have slept fitfully, but the narrow bed was welcoming and soft, despite the twanging of the bed springs. I fell deep asleep.

# Unbeknownst to His Holiness

**duplicity**. The practice of being two-faced,
of dishonestly acting in two opposing ways;
deceitfulness; double-dealing.
— *Oxford English Dictionary*

THE NEXT DAY FOLLUM AND I were issued our plastic-covered passes for the electric gates at the Schloss Issel offices, clipping them onto our shirt pockets. When I asked directions, the security sergeant motioned in the direction of the Historical Section, a long walk past the other iron gates. Counter-Sabotage, Counter-Espionage, Technical Operations, Covert Operations, Communications, Code Room and finally the Historical Section.

Captain McQuire, a tall woman in her late thirties with close-cropped red hair and a well-pressed uniform, came to open the gate for us. She wore the perfectly round, Army-issue eye glasses. I noticed among her medals the Expert Rifleman's Badge, as well as the Airborne Paratroopers wings. She waved us into the Historical Section, a long room with desks in rows, a green-shaded study lamp at each desk, men and women facing away from the casement windows. Those in civilian clothes were as numerous as those in Army uniforms, and all the eyes turned to inspect us.

She said, "Welcome, men, you're just in time. MacIntosh and Bloomberg left for stateside yesterday, so you'll take their desks, forty and forty-one. We're in the middle of a great project here, not unlike the Doomsday Book. We report on people rather than estates, though. We document every known European spy since the war, what he did, why he did it, and who he did it with. Our group is pulling it all together, one dossier at a time."

I asked, "So we write the entries?"

She nodded. "When this is done, staff everywhere can cross-reference by place or name, instantly find the data they need, compressed into several volumes. Every command will have a copy. We have a vast resource here, the Central Registry, but have not used it effectively until now. You both have Top Secret clearance, I see, and Bradford, the Sharp-Shooters Badge. Never know when a fellow might need that. Callard, here, will show you the ropes."

She walked away from us with her clipboard pressed to her flat bosom. There was no conversation in the room, only the hush and paper-rustling of a large university library. I could hear my mother. *Little you would know of library sounds; rustling, indeed.*

Callard was a tall man, a Corporal by his stripes, with bad complexion. Despite his years, only a few more than me, he had thinning blond hair, a Dickensian stooped posture, and his blue eyes moved past us and flickered around the room as he talked. It was clear that he was bright, curious about the world, and that he was fully able to consider more than one idea at a time. His voice was soft and nuanced.

"So many bad people to write about in Europe today. We've divided it into sectors, fifty of them and you'll each get a sector. You'll note how things seem to get more evil as you go south and east, the most evil in Vienna. Let me see, you're Bradford, desk forty, and will work on the Austrian desk with Countess von Kravitz, and Follum, desk forty-one. Don't look so worried, sweetheart, you're Czechoslovakia with the countess, too. Follow me."

We walked out the gate and up the stairs to the Central Registry, the entire top two floors of the schloss. Every room on both floors, perhaps fifty of them, was filled with filing cabinets, narrow rows going every which way between them, arrowed signs like road directions at each door pointing to dossier numbers. Six hundred thousands this way, eight hundred thousands that way. Russia to the left, Czechoslovakia straight ahead.

"I haven't counted them myself, mind you, but McQuire says there are over a million dossiers here. A through J from Berlin, H to Z from Vienna. In London, the British have K through S from Berlin, and the Russians have everything else. The big boys divvied them up in the last days of the war. It was a grab bag. We also have all our own dossiers. And the ones we bought from the Vatican."

"Why the Vatican?" I asked.

"McQuire says that certain cardinals in nineteen forty-six needed money for new robes, theirs all tatty from the war. One night those naughty girls sold us copies of thirty thousand dossiers, a dollar each, unbeknownst to his holiness."

As we walked up the stairs to the Central Registry, Callard told us more about our dealings at the Holy City. The good prelates sold the same dossiers to the British, the French, the Canadians, the East Germans, Lichtenstein and separately to the Russians, each sale in small denomination American dollars only, *per favore*. The tailors and shoemakers on the narrow streets near the Vatican were kept busy for months making new crimson pumps and sewing up the full-skirted red robes.

Callard explained the registry system of dossier numbers

and locating them in the upstairs warren. A list pasted on each drawer showed the missing dossiers, ones currently being read with a desk number following.

Follum asked, "How do we know where to start?"

"Katherine, the Countess Kravitz, will direct you. The project is like a huge piece of crochet, one strand connecting to another, to another, to another. An antimacassar of secrets. Only a small number of people know the grand scheme, how these all fit together. McQuire, Katherine, and a few others."

Follum said, "I guess I understand."

Callard said, "We're like that family who paints the Golden Gate Bridge again and again; we will never be done but what we need start again. To add to the confusion, people come and go, men get reassigned just as they become expert on the Salzburg cabal or the Red Professors at Tübingen. Draftees, when their time is up, get to go home in the very middle of a dossier, leaving it open on the desk for the next person."

In the weeks that followed, I understood more about Callard's offhand description of our mission. It was an endless pursuit, references here crossing over to other citations, new names and sometimes, folding back upon itself when a formerly-read dossier popped up again. If we were the lowest caste at the schloss, at least the chairs were comfortable.

I thought of the monks in the monasteries on Irish headlands and their years of writing scrolls in the gray light until their ink-stained fingers were so crippled that they could only hold a quill, nothing else. What did you do with your life, Brother Harold, how did you make a difference? I wrote mostly the small black letters but sometimes the large red ones or the gold-leafed borders. The gold-leaf days were good days.

# Gorgeous Merchandise

I'll trade you for your candy,
some gorgeous merchandise,
My camera, it's a dandy,
six by nine, just your size.
You want my porcelain figure? Black Market...
— *Marlene Dietrich*


CORPORAL MURGON CAUGHT up with me for his guideline lecture on life at Schloss Issel, as Sergeant-Major Tetley had requested. He came over to my table at the Bierstube Langenscheidt, across the street from the schloss, while I was waiting for Follum.

The corporal was slight and dark. He sat down without being asked and looked both ways at the other stube customers before he started to speak.

"Sergeant-Major asked me to get you up to speed. About Schloss Issel."

"Thanks, corporal, but I've already been here a couple of weeks now. Mostly I figured things out for myself."

But the corporal would not be stopped. "Don't come here very often to the Bierstube Langenscheidt, the higher-ups notice if a new enlisted man drinks too much. Don't miss the morning formation, and stay under the radar when it comes to leave requests. They watch men who take took much time off."

I said, "I'm looking forward to my leave time. Paris, maybe, or London."

"I would stick around here. Foreign travel is suspect."

"Callard goes to France a lot, he told me."

"I would especially avoid Callard, if I were you. He used to work with us in the Counterespionage, but high command transferred him over to Historical Section. We can't have any questionables in Counterespionage, you know."

I said, "I'm assigned to the Historical Section, too."

"Oh, well."

"Now, exactly what's wrong with Callard?"

It was obvious that Murgon relished passing along gossip and I could not help thinking of him as a fishmonger's wife, sleeves rolled to the elbows, trafficking poisonous stories as she wrapped the glassy-eyed purchase in newspaper. We new arrivals were the only ears that would listen, I was sure.

He said, "Callard is smart, I'll give him that. Phi Beta Kappa from Idaho, Master's Thesis almost done when he enlisted rather than being drafted. He can type faster than anybody else with no mistakes."

"That doesn't sound so bad."

"There's talk that he's a fairy. Nothing definite, but all the signs are there. Goes to the ballet and the opera, drinks late at night down in the Polish Quarter."

"All major crimes, I can see."

"If you're not going to take me seriously, I won't continue."

"Sorry, Murgon, but I go to concerts and the opera, too."

"Well, you're different from Callard, I can tell. He even makes a point to dress like the Germans, so he won't be picked out as an American. There is definitely something wrong with that."

"So a season ticket to the ballet and civilian clothes are damning evidence for Callard?"

"You'll see. Just wait."

Follum came to join us, but before he could say a word, I took the opportunity to leave Murgon and his tittle-tattle. "Eric, let's go over to the club. I said I would meet Callard. Thanks for everything, Murgon."

He glared at me as we left. As we crossed the street, Follum said, "I don't like him much, that Murgon."

"Creepy guy."

A few nights later, I walked down to Callard's room at the far end of the third floor. He had showered for the evening, dressed in slim black trousers and a black silk shirt. There was a towel around his neck, protecting his shirt while he patted a gooey substance around his eyes. A glass ampoule broken into halves stood beside the plate of goo on his footlocker.

"Belgian Elixir, Bradford. My friend Omer, the Brussels pianist at the TubeBar, smuggled a few ampoules into my pocket the other night. No mere soldier could afford them. I will, in time, give him favors in return. After five minutes on your face, he said, the elixir erases every sign of a crows-foot and those horrid marionette-mouth lines. I'll be a teen-ager again."

"Callard, you already look like a teen-ager, if a slightly wasted one."

"I know, but it pays to make sure on a night like tonight. The magic lasts until midnight, though, so fast work is required. I wish you could see what will happen, but I can't take you with me tonight."

"You don't look old."

"Tonight, I definitely won't. Every eye on my entrance to the Krakow Klub, where I pause for a moment to let the cold night air swirl about me, heads turning as snow eddies into the room. Then, cruel workers' hands reach to touch me as I pass by their rough tables, all the men engorged with desire and, at last, walking ever so slowly, giving savor to every eye, I reach my chair at the regulars' table, the *Stammtisch*, in the very middle of the Corps de Ballet. The whole table of handsome Polish regulars, the very heart of the ballet, stands with light applause, companionable hugs all around. Darling, how young you look. Herr Callard, so thin and hungry. *Guten Abend, Liebchen.* Sweaty bodies, joy beyond belief."

"All this from a Belgian goo?"

"Don't be snippy. You can come next time."

"I'm not sure I want to come."

"You do in your heart."

"It scares me a bit, your night world."

"You'll be my young apprentice, watching my every move. With the maestro, there will be no danger."

"We'll see, Callard."

He wiped away the excess ointment to reveal a startled look on his face, as if someone had clapped together a pair of pot lids behind his back. The Belgian astringent was working, but perhaps concocted with too heavy a hand.

As he walked away down the hall with his curious, almost sideways walk, he looked back over his shoulder and adjusted his black jacket and long scarf. The black beret finished his look, decidedly un-American and non-military. Four hours of bliss, then I turn into a sewer rat, he said; he dipped ever so slightly and rounded the corner.

The men of the Polish quarter were in for a surprise tonight. Or not.

The next day at lunch, Callard had recovered enough for conversation and he motioned for Follum and me to sit with him. Most of the other enlisted men shunned Callard's table because of his gamey talk and tainted reputation. Murgon was the source of his bad standing, I was sure.

"I had the most amazing offer at the Krakow Klub last night," he said.

Follum said, "Are you sure we want to hear?"

"Nothing salacious, Follum. There was this old woman at the *Stammtisch*, a Nazi widow, who reached across the table. She grabbed my hand in both of hers and said that I resembled her son, Manfred, dead at Stalingrad. So young, so sad." He put his own hand to the side of his face, now relaxed from the rigors of Belgium.

I said, "So the elixir was already paying dividends."

"She was most pleasant, smiling, talking to her companions about the resemblance."

I asked, "So what was her offer?"

"Don't rush me. I could understand a little of what she said to her friends as they all nodded their heads, but then she switched to English. Spoke it well. She asked me if I had an auto. All young men needed an automobile now, for their sweeties on the other side of town."

"She offered you her car?"

"No, it was her son's Mercedes. A nineteen thirty-seven four-door sedan with 'Wasserford' bud-vases. She bought it for him on his nineteenth birthday, pulling in favors owed his father, a high-ranking bureaucrat. Now it sits in her garage, nobody using it. Father and son both dead. "

"Is a Wasserford vase really Waterford vase?"

"I think so. She mentioned the bud-vases several times, *Englischerkristal für die blumen*, she said. *Sehr schön.*"

She's going to *give* the Mercedes to you?"

"She will sell it to me, a very cheap price for her son. For Stalingrad. It does her no good there in the garage, gives her the bad memories every week when she starts the engine, to make sure it still runs."

"How much?"

"A thousand Deutsch Marks. I immediately said yes, a thousand thanks, Frau Mueller."

"That's two hundred fifty dollars. Do you have that?"

"No, of course not, but I have an idea." He put his finger to his lips and looked sideways.

Callard's scheme was to sell cigarettes on the Black Market. We all knew that there was an active exchange in the village nights of Bad Issel. A carton of cigarettes, for which we paid one dollar at the PX, brought ten dollars down in the village. That was forty Deutsch Marks. We only needed to sell ten cartons, he said.

Follum said, "But that's only four hundred marks."

Callard answered, "I have a little tucked away from another enterprise."

I said, "I don't want to be involved in the Black Market, Callard. And I speak for Follum, too. It's highly illegal and too risky. A life sentence in the stockade."

"No problem, my betters taught me how to disappear into walls when needed, to blend with the night, to creep around the corner. I'll do all the undercover work. Just buy me your monthly allotment of four cartons each. I'll use two from my allotment, and, there we have it, four hundred marks plus my stash makes a thousand."

Weeks ago Follum and I had talked about how it would be to have a car, to be able to drive away from Bad Issel on weekends, but an enlisted man could not make a dent in such a purchase. My pay was sixty dollars a month, Follum's fifty-five. Here was the possibility of partial ownership, just for giving up the cigarettes that neither of us smoked.

I said, "Callard, we'll do it for full half-ownership, a quarter for Follum and a quarter for me."

"Where did you learn to bargain, Bradford? So harshly with such a dear friend? Very unlike what I know of other gentle West Texans."

I knew that now was the time to press our advantage. "Half the time we get to use the car without you. Fair?"

He considered for a few seconds, then said, "Fair."

We bought our month's quota of cigarettes the next week-end and gave them to Callard. He reported back later about his dealings in Bad Issel. He asked around the village fountain before taking any cigarettes down there. An old man told him that the market was designed to confuse the authorities, to make a trail the *polizei* cannot follow.

A potential seller went into the Issel Stube and ordered a glass of beer, asking if the accordionist could play the third verse of Lilli Marlene. This signaled that there were three cartons for sale. The fifth verse would mean five cartons. The waitress would be shocked and say it was forbidden to play that song, but she would ask. If the market was in operation that night, she said yes when she returned with the beer, *Alles ist gut.* Of course, the accordionist would not really play it.

Then, after a spell, the seller walked outside and across to the village fountain where a woman with a cane sat waiting. Without breaking stride, he must deposit his cartons, wrapped in brown paper, into the shoulder-bag that she briefly opened. The seller continued on quickly away in the opposite direction from the woman, who hobbled off with her fat satchel safely under one arm. This led the seller to the church door, deep-set and in the shadows, where a man or perhaps another woman paid him thirty marks. They parted without conversing. If other people loitered around the fountain, there would be no market. If there was a full moon, there would be no market.

Callard said, "It took me four trips up and down the hill, but here it all is." He had a stack of mark notes, our contribution and his own. Follum went with Callard on Sunday to buy the Mercedes from the widow in case his mechanic's expertise might be needed to get it going again. By late afternoon, they pulled into the usually vacant slot marked "Enlisted Parking" in the forecourt of Schloss Issel. They had detoured by the Bad Issel cemetery to snip the last of autumn's roses, now fragrant in the bud-vases. We drove triumphantly around Bad Issel, turning on and off the headlights in full daylight, running the windshield wipers on dry glass and lightly honking the horn.

He said, "I told Frau Mueller that the vases would always have roses for Stalingrad. Tonight I will drive to the Krakow Klub. All my dear Polskis will come out to the curb and admire. I'll have my absolute pick."

I said, "Don't forget, half the time is for Follum and me."

"Such a waste. The pride of Stuttgart could be yours with a single honk."

"Drive carefully, Callard. We want our half back, undented."

# Flecks of Crimson

> But don't go into Mr. McGregor's garden:
> your Father had an accident there;
> he was put into a pie by Mrs. McGregor.
> — *Beatrix Potter*

CAPTAIN MCQUIRE ASKED, "DO you have a sport jacket and a pair of slacks, Bradford? Ones that you brought from stateside when you came?"

"Yes, ma'am"

"Do you have plans for the week-end?"

Even though I feared that the McQuire was asking me out for a social event, I told her no. I hoped it was not a reception at the consulate, thin-lipped functionaries in the overheated salons or a concert performance of Wagner going on past midnight. Everybody knew that McQuire loved music and missed little of importance at the concert hall.

"Splendid, then. We'll courier some documents to Zurich, down there on Saturday, back by Sunday morning. You know about courier duty, don't you, Bradford?"

"Somewhat, ma'am. But not all the details."

"I'll catch you up on the train. Be ready to leave at o-eight-hundred on Saturday. Wear your jacket and slacks, and a tie. No suitcase, no identity papers, no laundry marks."

That sounded ominous; nothing to identify the body. What I did know about courier duty was limited. Communications in Europe in 1957 were unreliable: telephone lines to Berlin went through Russian-held East Germany and were presumed to be tapped at multiple locations. Lines south to Switzerland could not be verified past Donaueschingen and those to France went through the Black Forest, where there were many opportunities for unwitnessed splicing. Any form of radio was impossible because scrambling devices could not be trusted. Important Army documents were required by regulation to be delivered by hand, an officer and at least one enlisted aide, two aides in matters of highest security. Couriers left Schloss Issel every day in all manner of dress, like centurions on horseback with rolled parchments from Rome.

That evening at the club I asked Callard about courier duty. He said that McQuire was annoyed with him after their trip to Luxembourg, so she had been trying out replacements. I was merely the newest replacement.

"Why was she annoyed?"

"I can't say. She's ruthless with her favorites; like Tiberius, she throws them over with the first flicker of boredom."

"I'll take care that the emperor is amused, then."

"Tread lightly near any cliff, my friend."

The next morning the plain gray sedan met us at 0800. McQuire was in civilian attire, a checkered black and white suit with a salamander brooch, brownish stockings, a black coat over her shoulders and a shiny black hat with a feather. In her military uniform, she appeared much younger. Now, she looked like a middle-aged Nebraskan on vacation, Miss Partridge on a schoolteachers' tour of the Swiss cantons.

She said, "Your checkered jacket and slacks are perfect. I

couldn't have found any as good in the Supply Room."

"I guess that's a compliment."

"Take it that way."

When I asked her a question about the assignment, she put her finger to her lips and pointed to the driver. We motored in silence to downtown Stuttgart to an iron-fenced house called Villa Ingrid. Very near to the Hauptbahnhof, it had survived the blanket bombings of the Allies. Gossip about Villa Ingrid lived a healthy life among the desks at the Historical Section.

We knew that it was involved with Hungarian matters, the debriefing of refugees from the revolution, training of agents, agendas for the future, but little more. Volunteers needed special clearances to work in the villa and assignment there was highly sought after. The steel driveway gate opened automatically and we drove into a bay of the garage, the driver closing the garage door before McQuire moved to get out.

A woman who resembled McQuire in stature met us at the garage door and took us to a room on the ground floor. There were two fake crocodile suitcases, medium-sized, on the center table. Without a word, McQuire took one and motioned for me to take the other. Mine was heavy. We walked through hallways with closed oak doors and out through the garden behind the villa. Unlike the front, the back garden had a large lawn, linden trees and a high wall with a gate, which buzzed open as we neared. We ducked out onto the back street, McQuire looking both ways. The street was empty and the boarded up back windows of adjacent villas were eyeless.

We walked the few blocks to the Hauptbahnhof and waited for the train to Zurich at 0935. On the bench in the large waiting hall she told me about the assignment.

"Switzerland is, on the surface, our ally, but they strongly forbid the US from covert operations or counterintelligence operations of any nature. To get secret documents to our offices in Zurich, we need to look like ordinary citizens on vacation, a mother and her son from Boston, or an aunt and her nephew, we'll have to decide which on the way there. I have your papers in my hand-bag."

"Will somebody meet us in Zurich?"

"No, we'll take the first taxi to the museum, talking all the time about modern art. The consulate is on the next street, so after the taxi leaves we'll walk around and leave our suitcases there. There will be identical suitcases waiting for us, packed with old clothes, which we will bring back to Bad Issel."

"Do you expect trouble?"

"We should always expect trouble."

I looked around at the other benches in the hall, red-cheeked Germans taking on a more sinister aspect with this new information. Germans often stared energetically at Americans, so that only added to my mistrust. It appeared that a woman all in black on a far bench was watching us without respite. Would a foreign agent not be trained to look away now and then? To stare was a dead giveaway. I was sure that McQuire had seen that danger in the black dress, but she did not deem it worth her comment.

"Don't get too spooked, Bradford, but we *will* be followed. It only remains to identify which of these seated are the ones. Usually more than one."

"Shouldn't we be armed?"

"I am, but you should hold tight to your suitcase."

"I thought that the Regular Army agents did this work, the ones with years of training."

"They do, but I prefer a new man like you. Intelligent amateurs, quick to respond to new stimulus, make the best couriers. There's something about a trained agent that gives them away. A tired nonchalance, I think, like priests who have heard too many confessions."

"Don't they recognize you after so many assignments?"

"I change my appearance each time."

This did nothing to allay my fears, because the captain looked just like the captain to me, even in her distinctive dress from Omaha. Surely the trained European eye, honed by centuries of intense observations, could see through her mid-American veneer.

A new thought popped into my mind.

"Has anybody been killed doing this?" I asked.

"Not in a long time."

Bowel-opening fear was not the proper response, so I said, "The sign-board says our train is boarding."

"Keep your eyes peeled."

At the gate, I looked back for the bench with the old woman in black, but she had moved forward to a few places behind us in the line. My knuckles must have been snow white on the suitcase handle. I wondered if I was really meant for courier duty. My dossier-covered desk with its green-shaded lamp seemed so homey, so safe, so far away, the monkish calligrapher's table with scrolls awaiting the pen, shelter from the buffetings of the world, no treacherous old women in black dresses and shoe-daggers washed in nerve poison.

I followed McQuire onto a second-class car; she walked through several more until she found a compartment already occupied by four young women, apparently school-girls. They moved to allow us to sit together.

McQuire put her suitcase on the rack above her head, so I did the same. The schoolgirls watched intently as I helped McQuire position hers. Just as we were seated, the train started to move. McQuire settled in with aplomb, shaking open a copy of the *Paris Herald Tribune*. In a few minutes I saw the old woman go by our compartment, turn her head to see us, pause slightly and then go on. McQuire, who was deep in the news columns, had not noticed. I suddenly had to pee, but expected I ought to wait.

McQuire introduced herself in German and asked where

the girls lived. *München*. Did they go to school there? *Ja*. Were they going on holiday? *Ja, ja, bestimmt*. Did they like to ski in Switzerland? *Natürlich, Fräulein*. Then followed a ten minute exchange of Teutonic chatter, McQuire and the girls nodding back and forth, smiling, laughing, in the end all turning to look at me.

"What?" I said.

"I just told the girls that you were my handsome nephew and studying to be an artist. *Ein Kunstler*."

It was a four hour trip to Zurich, with a short stop at the border. The old woman came by our compartment several times, once stopping without shame to look straight in at me as the four girls and McQuire dozed. A cold winter rain devoid of compassion fell on me when she stared, her eyes near enough to mine to see their ice-blue color. Were those flecks of crimson in the blue? I wondered if she had a gun in the handbag that she clutched to her breast. Perhaps there was a special grommet hole in the leather and the gun was already aimed right at my nose. The silenced bullet would go straight through the grommet, not even scratching the weathered leather of her handbag, and slip through the window glass while my compartment companions slept. I was a dead man, I knew, but then she lowered the bag and moved on. The fear resounded in me for the next hour like a billiard ball caroming aimlessly from side to side, side to side.

At the border, the Swiss Customs men walked the car inspecting each passport in turn. McQuire produced ours from her bag and they nodded, asked her something in German, but she replied in English.

"I don't speak good German. My nephew and I will be staying in Zurich only long enough for the museum. Thank you." The girls looked at her strangely as they offered their papers, because the Fraülein spoke acceptable German. They knew something was amiss. I remembered a caveat from intelligence school: never speak a foreign language at borders, only English, even if you were multi-fluent. McQuire must have hundreds of these guidelines available for instant use, ready to wend our way through difficulties.

The customs men considered what she said, looked back at our passports, stamped them and closed our compartment door. In Zurich, everything went as planned. After being deposited at the *Kunstmuseum*, we strolled along an avenue with horse-chestnut trees and turned into a side street. There was a Marine at the consulate gate; he looked at McQuire's passports, let us in immediately.

After the exchange of suitcases, McQuire led us to the Grand Hotel au Lac for a late lunch. The Stuttgart train did not depart until 1700. I could feel my knuckles more relaxed on the lighter replacement suitcase full of somebody's shirts and socks. We were seated at a table with a view of the lake, where small steamboats arrived and departed, tight squadrons of black swans moving in and out of their way.

"Bradford, it went well."

"I was sure that old woman had a gun in her purse."

"What old woman?"

"The one who kept looking into our compartment. All in black."

"Don't let your artist's imagination get the better of you."

"I'm sure she wasn't just another old lady."

"Europe is full of old ladies in black."

"But this one had the eyes of a killer. Flecks of crimson, I'm sure."

"What nonsense. Let's order our lunch."

Perhaps she was right. I was too suggestive, too easy to unnerve. She ordered for us both while I tried to translate the menu. *Lendenschnitte mit Anana*. Mixed vegetables and *Bratkartofflen*. Coffee and thin slices of Munster Cheese for dessert. The knot that had been tying and retying itself behind my ear loosened a bit and gave me the first sense of well-being since we left Schloss Issel. Then I looked over McQuire's shoulder to see the same woman in black at a far table, looking our way.

"Captain..." I started.

"Call me Aunty, Bradford."

"Aunty, there's the woman I told you about right at a table behind you. The woman in black."

"Can I turn around? Is she looking?"

"She's always looking."

"Well, then it won't matter." She put on her glasses and turned around as only another woman can, moving her focus from table to table, slightly forward to an earlier table, then backwards, slowly backwards, not missing a single face, appearing to be propelled merely by a simple, sociable curiosity, until it landed on the old woman, almost directly behind McQuire. Some of the other women at tables in the restaurant secretly observed McQuire's sweep with admiration. No man could have executed that circular camera movement with such bravura. McQuire nodded to the old woman. The old woman nodded back.

"Bradford, she's one of ours. Works downtown as an analyst in the Villa Ingrid, but a killer in her own right."

"You didn't tell me. What's her name?"

"There's no need for you to know."

"So, she followed us?"

"Our back-up. Those papers in the suitcases must have been really important."

"Is that a machine gun in her purse?"

"Something very like it. Let's see if we can get some more coffee."

I lost sight of the Villa Ingrid woman on the return. No doubt it was not so urgent to protect our suitcases on this trip, so she would be sleeping with her feet up in another compartment, snoring with the machine-gunned purse under her elbows on her lap. Europe was a much more dangerous place than most people imagined. The gray car met us at the Stuttgart station and drove us without conversation to Schloss Issel.

As it departed, McQuire said, "You're tightly wired, Bradford. Not a bad quality overall for courier duty."

"Thanks, ma'am. I won't be so nervous on the next assignment."

"Good, because there will be more, I can assure you." So Tiberius had picked a new favorite. Me. I made a note to be careful where I walked.

I said, "It would be nice if it weren't on a weekend every time, though."

She looked at me without expression, but did not answer me. Had I already displeased her?

"Just a thought, ma'am."

Did my days as the favorite, luncheons by the lake with stemmed glasses of white wine and *Lendenschnitte,* promise to be short or had I built a rapport with the captain, partners in the shepherding of secrets across a malevolent Europe?

# SUFFUSION

*Such romantic illusions, and they're all about you.*
*— Marlene Dietrich*

"WE'LL ONLY STAY FOUR OR FIVE days. Sarah called and said she needed to see me. Asked for you to come, too. We can swim, drink some beers, go frog-gigging."

A road trip always excited Henry Zilbert, away from Middleton for a week or so. He asked me to take off work, join him on the trek over to Parthenon. In the years before he had invited me several times but I turned him down because of my summer work.

I said, "Yesterday I was fired from the highway department. Dad got the job for me. Your father is a good man, they said, but there's no place here for you, Bradford. I'll cash this last check on the way out of town."

"Don't bring much. Shirts, pants, swimming suit."

A stop by the house to pack, on to the bank and we were on the road by late morning. The drive from Middleton in West Texas to Parthenon in far East Texas took seven hours on the farm-to-market roads, no stopping. We talked little as we drove through San Angelo, Robert Lee, Goldthwaite, Brownwood, across the middle of Texas to Nacogdoches, Chireno and finally the last half hour into Parthenon, where Sarah, Henry's grandmother, lived.

This was a year before I was drafted, Henry Zilbert and I home for the summer. Before Schloss Issel. We shared a room at college for the last three years. Summers brought us back to Middleton, he to help his grandfather on the ranch and I for temporary work in the oil fields or the pipeline. It would be best to let Dad cool down about my being sacked at the highway department. When we got back I would need to avoid family dinners for a while.

Just outside of Parthenon we turned off into the Blanchett Farm, a gravel road crowded by magnolia trees in a long crescent, dark leaves brushing against the car. I rolled down the window on the passenger side and the moist smell of evening pastures flowed in like water. Honeysuckle, magnolia, new-mown hay and turned earth. It was barely light, the sky a dark violet blue. Around the curve, we saw Sarah's house, a clapboard two-story with yellowish light filling the double-hung windows.

Sarah had not set foot in Middleton since her son, Henry's father, was killed in the war, counseling the family with detailed letters and, more recently, telephone calls. Henry's grandfather refused to go to Parthenon, she would not come back to Middleton, and so the Zilberts had lived apart for twenty years. Sarah was there to meet us at the door.

"I love you, Henry John. Do you know that?" She was tall enough to kiss him on the forehead, like a favored son. With a sense of personal style that we saw little of in Middleton, she wore pleated ivory slacks, a black-and-white striped blouse, and a black silk scarf tucked around her neckline. Her hair was pure white, abundant, cut sharply short and straight. She and Henry had the same burnt-umber eyes. Sarah bought her clothes in New York, Henry had told me, not trusting Dallas to have what she wanted.

"Yes, ma'am. You remember Harold."

"I do. Come in, both of you. Francie's gone for the night, but she left some cold chicken and potato salad in the kitchen." It was cooler in the house, a lingering mix of aromas: cooking, cut-flowers and damp fabric.

Henry said, "We ate in Nacogdoches. No need."

"You talk like Henry Sr. Not a spare word. Harold, are *you* hungry?"

"No, ma'am."

"Henry John can 'ma'am' me, but you call me Sarah, please. If Francie's chicken doesn't suit, at least get yourselves a cold beer." She pronounced her name Say-rah.

After twenty minutes of conversation between Henry and Sarah about Middleton — who was still there, what the Zilbert neighbors were up to, how the Angus herd was doing — we went up to bed. Henry and I were staying in Sarah's father's room, which she said had the best view of the pastures. Twin beds now stood where Earl Blanchett's four-poster bed almost touched the ceiling. Francie would serve breakfast on the lawn about eight.

A cool breeze came through the windows, laboring to break up the moist heat inside. I slept under a half a sheet, fitfully in the warmth. At first light, I got up and took a shower, dressed in clean Levis and a button-down shirt. Henry did not stir. On the back lawn, Sarah was already having coffee at a narrow table, reading a newspaper.

"Join me, Harold. I have a hot carafe here." She poured me a cup and folded her newspaper. The morning air was cooler, but sultry.

I said, "This is beautiful. So different from Middleton, so green." We looked across the rolling Blanchett fields to the native hardwoods of East Texas: oaks, maples, dogwoods, wild cherries and tulip trees, making a dark verge. Compared to the dry openness of West Texas, it was a close green paradise, ponds brimming, streams rushing into all of the low places, sounds of tree frogs and water birds.

She said, "These were cotton fields in the last century, but we turned them to permanent pasture years ago. A cattle *farm* instead of a ranch. We make three cuttings of hay for winter feed, have open pasture the rest of the summer. I can call the cows from here. We don't brand them. Pets, almost. Not like the wild, tough cattle on the Zilbert spread."

"Henry loves that ranch."

"I know, just like his grandfather. He thought that good-for-nothing Middleton spread was the land of Goshen. It is all your Henry John's now that Henry Sr. has passed."

It was difficult for me to call her Sarah. "Sarah, Henry said that you were born here?"

She nodded, "When the tobacco failed in the eighteen forties, the brave part of the family came west, founded Parthenon. The worried ones stayed on in Virginia, getting fatter and more fretful. Lots of Blanchett cousins around here, first, second and twice-removed cousins. It's always been home for me."

"I can see why you like it."

"I wish I could get Henry John to like it, too, to sell up and move here. We have two farms still in the family that he could have, the Grand Vert and the Yellowwood, either one. But I think he's got too much Zilbert blood. Dry-land, Zilbert blood."

"You never know."

Henry walked out and joined us. Sarah poured him a cup of coffee and refilled mine. Francie, a thin, straight-boned black woman, brought eggs, biscuits, butter and bacon. Sarah touched her arm gently and looked up to thank her.

Sarah said to Henry, "We've been talking about your selling up and moving back to Parthenon. Francie's chicken dinners every Friday night. What do you think, Henry John?"

"What did Harold say?"

"Very little. He's a smart young man."

Henry said, "We have our friends back in Middleton. Harold and I talk about sharing the house on Water Street, living together."

She said, "So you should live together, but I never liked that house. Your great-grandfather Zilbert had a heavy hand with it, brown woodwork, dark plaster and those pier glasses."

"It's the oldest house on Water Street."

"Henry John, if you won't come back here to Parthenon, you should pull it right down and build a new house. A modern house for two bachelors with a swimming pool in the back garden. Get a good architect from Dallas."

He tried to ignore his grandmother. He said, "As it is, Harold can use the attic for his studio, and I will run the ranch from there. In town. Convenient, central."

"Harold, wouldn't you like a proper studio with a big north window, no dusty old attic, where that garage is now, and a long pool to have your friends over?"

Henry replied before I could. "Sarah, leave off. The house is fine just the way it is. Harold and I can move right in when we graduate next May."

She said, "I give up, then. What about the Army?"

"We went by the bank and John Bartram said the war will be over in a few months, no more draft."

"John Bartram is quite often dead wrong."

"He said to send his love. How's that pretty thing, your Sarah?"

"Did he now?"

Later that morning, Henry and I drove Sarah into Parthenon, three miles east of the farm. With the convertible top down, we circled the court-house, which she said was a scaled copy of the Temple of Zeus in Greece. On adjoining streets, canopied with live oaks and Chinaberry trees full of blackbirds, there were other Classic Revival houses with Doric porches, windows with pediments and the invariable green shutters, some angling away from their hinges. The more imposing houses were the Blanchett cousins, she said, and the others were owned by newcomers who bought in after the War.

I thought that Parthenon had a caught-in-amber quality, curious green amber, a town waiting for the world to press in, to make changes. Changes that might not prosper under Chinaberry trees.

I asked, "Are there oilfields near Parthenon?"

She said, "No, north and east of here, near Tyler. A little shallow sweet near Chireno. We just have the farmland and the timber around here. No royalty checks."

Henry said, "Humble Oil is drilling next to the ranch in Martin County right now. We might just get a lot of royalty on that good-for-nothing Zilbert land."

"Don't be smart to your grandmother, son. You're as much a Blanchett as a Zilbert."

"Just joking, Sarah."

"I miss you, Henry John. Why can't you be here all the time?"

"I'll try to come more now that college is about over."

She said, "I don't have many more really good years."

"I know."

The next morning, Sarah and I drank our cups of coffee before Henry came down. There was a faint breeze against the hot press of morning. Looking away across the field to the forest, she put her hand over on mine. It was smooth and cool.

"Don't get caught up in Henry John's good looks, Harold, like I did with his grandfather. A fly stuck in honey."

I said, "I think he *is* handsome, Sarah. I wish I had his dark hair, brown eyes."

"Henry Sr. could turn heads on the streets of Middleton. Every woman had hungry eyes for him, but all he wanted was that old, dry land. And me, he said. He was always loyal to me."

"You never liked the ranch?"

"I did in the early years with summer rains. The grass grew up to the stirrups and went as far as the eye could see. I fancied that it was the steppes of Mother Russia when we rode out for roundups. Then the dust started to blow year after year. We talked about selling up and moving east. But Henry Sr. was afraid he would lose his soul here in Parthenon, be the worthless son-in-law of rich, old Earl Blanchett. It's true that Papa never liked him much. If Henry Sr. stayed hundreds of miles away in Middleton, he could still be his own man."

"I can see that."

"Harold, you will also have to fight to be yourself, to be a painter. The Zilberts are beguiling, can trap you in what passes for love. Henry John is very fond of you, but he is a Zilbert, stubborn, manly, unbending."

"I think that's why I like him."

"Big mistake, unless you want to be suffused by Henry John, nothing for yourself."

"I don't know what I want." I knew that Sarah was right, but I hoped that the summer days would just go on. We could stay ever as young men, extending our college days into bachelorhood, drinking too much, avoiding plans of any sort. Being suffused by Henry did not sound like a bad thing at all.

He joined us at the breakfast table. Our heresy must have been written on our faces. He said, "What have you been talking about? Me?"

Sarah said, "Guilty."

After breakfast, Henry and I went swimming in the lake just beyond Parthenon, bog water clear as brown glass. Rounding a bend, we swam way out, not talking above the splash of our arms. Climbing up the ladder to the raft moored in the middle of the lake, we lay down in the sun.

I said, "Sarah thinks I love you too much."

"Do you?"

"She says I will become a part of you, get filled by you and that I won't be myself. I'll have to fight to be a separate person, an artist."

"That doesn't sound so bad," he said.

"I thought so, too. To become saturated with you, permeated by you. It gets me excited to just think about it."

"Sarah can complicate things." Henry took off his swimming shorts and I saw as he turned toward me that he was as aroused as I was. I pulled him close and kissed him, my hand stroking him gently. I could that see his brown eyes were open, looking past me. Sarah knew there was an attraction between us, but she got it wrong by one hundred and eighty degrees. I was the one who would take Henry, make him give in to me. Henry John, the dark brooding manly one, was just about to get himself suffused by the artistic one. The buzzing sound of an outboard motor around the bend stopped us cold. We hustled back into our trunks and down into the water. The outboard went past us and turned down into another inlet as we swam back to shore. Henry came close to me and returned a long kiss while the cars went back and forth on the pond road.

He said, "Let's not forget this back on Water Street."

But we would forget. That night at dinner, Sarah saw that something had happened because she looked at me in a different way. It was as if I had become larger or taller, a change she would now have to deal with. She was charming to me, solicitous of Henry. Francie brought in a dessert soufflé, portioned it between us on rose-painted plates. Sarah raised her glass of iced water as if it were wine.

"I have a sort of toast to make. Henry John, the Grand Vert farm is yours now if you will come and live there with Harold. We can build him a north-facing studio, get you some farm machinery, maybe even a swimming pool. I will have the papers drawn up tomorrow in town."

Henry said, "Why now, Sarah? Why give it to me now?"

"Because I fear for the two of you on Water Street, never growing up, never coming back here to Parthenon. Middleton's dusty power will take hold of you, pull you in like it did Henry Sr. If you have an obligation here, a home for both of you, maybe that won't happen."

He said, "Won't the farm come to me in your will?"

"That could be a long while down the line. Even if I feel poorly at times, Blanchetts tend to live into their nineties, testy and frail. And, who knows, I might give it all to the church. The new pastor at St. Bede's has come calling, talking about a thirty-foot rose window for Big Earl and a permanent endowment for an English choirmaster."

Henry said, "Thanks Sarah, but let me think about it. Back in Middleton, in the house with the brown woodwork. It's hard for me to make sense here."

From what I knew of Henry, he had already thought about it, made sense of it. As we drove on the two-lane roads back to Middleton, we talked about other things as the green amber faded into the drier air. The promise of sensual adventure that teased us at the pond never took root in the hardscrabble acres of Martin County, even on the nights when we drank too much and watched the dawn. I kept the hope that we would make our love in the near future, that it would happen by itself.

But the ranch had a thirty-year mortgage on Henry, a long-term obligation with no hope of an early payoff. On snowy nights in Bad Issel, I still wondered what might have happened if he did not spurn the rolling fields of Parthenon, eating Francie's chicken dinners and lemon soufflés over at Sarah's, spending warm nights with me in the upper bedroom at Grand Vert, Big Earl looking down upon us without amusement.

# PLUM BLOSSOMS FALLING

> Forgive, O Lord, my little jokes on Thee
> and I'll forgive Thy great big one on me.
> — *Robert Frost*

THE EBB AND FLOW OF THE DAYS at Schloss Issel insulated me from the matters of real concern in the outside world. Politics, presidential speeches, hydrogen explosions in Polynesia and unrest in Algeria were of no matter. Follum and I had become accustomed to walking across the street from the schloss to the Bierstube Langenscheidt after dinner. Corporal Murgon sat by himself at a small table, wary of being associated with friends of Callard. I felt comfortable with Follum, as if we had grown up together. We nursed two or three beers in as many hours, talked, looked idly at the other beer-drinkers, German civilians and American army, who looked idly back.

After a long stretch of silence, Follum said, "I wrote my girl friend, Melanie Petersen, about life here, how exciting it is."

"This is exciting?"

"For a man who wants to be a music director, Germany is

the land of Beethoven, Bach and the grand cathedral organs. It is exciting to be so near to Bonn and Ulm. My professors at college said that the high notes from the organ in Ulm take a full ten seconds to die out."

"I'll try to understand that as exciting. We should take a trip to Ulm, Eric. Soon. We're getting behind on our Mercedes hours."

He continued, "I'd like that. I also wrote that I've met this artist named Bradford; how we've become friends and talked every night over beer. Melanie loves museums and paintings, and she wants you to promise to be in our wedding, after we all get home."

"I would love to be in your wedding, Follum."

"I knew that, but there's something else."

"She wants to come over here to get married?"

"No. She's sensible and definitely prefers to wait, Bradford. Melanie wants *you* to paint my portrait."

"I'm not really good at portraits, Follum."

"Melanie said you would say that."

"I can try. No guarantees, though."

We agreed to start on the week-end. I earlier had found an art supply store in Stuttgart and put together all the supplies in my wall locker. After morning formation was dismissed, we set up a chair next to the easel in my quarters. My roommates were off together on a trip to Heidelberg, so we had the morning to ourselves.

I mulled the portrait over in my mind since Follum asked about it and I decided upon a front view of his face and shoulders. It would be like the pioneer ancestor portraits you see in family sitting rooms, nothing fancy or self-consciously arty, but a modern version of the naïve paintings that I imagined must be on every Wisconsin wall. Since Follum was a light-haired Norwegian, I chose a background nearly the same pale-yellow color as his abundant hair. It would enhance his complexion, the natural light from the windows coming from his left.

The portraits I had painted before were disappointments for me and most for the sitters, as well, so I wondered why I had agreed to this one so readily. Perhaps Follum's classic looks made the decision for me.

"Just sit still and look slightly off to your left. Not at me."

"Like this?"

"Perfect." The charcoal stick drawing went quickly, so I opted to go right into the painted version, to keep the momentum. First the shadows in an umber wash, then the mid-tones for the face. The drawing showed through the wash; with highlights and fine-tuning yet to come; the likeness was striking. I reworked the face slightly, widening it where I had cast it too narrow. Follum was starting to move uneasily.

"Don't wiggle, Follum. Let me get this right."

"I'm not good at this."

"I'm not either, but you'll have to stay still. Think about something else. Tell me where you met your Melanie."

"I've known her all my life. The Petersens own the farm next to ours, a thousand acres."

"Somehow I don't see you as a married man."

"Why not? Everybody gets married in Wisconsin."

"Children? PTA? A mortgage?"

"It's what Melanie wants."

"Don't move your head as you talk. So the two of you played together as children?"

"We didn't have time for play, Bradford, like you over-sexed West Texas boys."

"Don't be defensive. You went to school and church with Melanie, saw her at Christmas get-togethers?"

"Yes. It was always set that Melanie and I would get married. We were the same age and not cousins. It was harder than you know to find a girl nearby who wasn't a cousin."

"But that's not as dangerous as everybody thinks. Eleanor and FDR were first cousins."

"Well, nobody in White Cloud would ever marry a cousin, even second cousins or once-removed cousins. There were so many stories about the deformed things that could happen."

"Pity that nobody warned the Roosevelts."

We kept up the talk while I painted until I reached a natural stopping place. The first day of the portrait had gone well. I knew better than to press on when I had reached a juncture. Follum came around to look at the canvas and stood in silence for half a minute.

He said, "Am I that good looking, Bradford?"

"The camera may lie, but the painter does not. *Artemis veritas* or something like that."

"Melanie will be happy, but my brothers probably won't."

"Why is that?"

"I was always the plain one of the Follum boys, good enough for the church, everybody said. His forehead is too high, eyes too far apart. He's too tall, and will have back problems later in life, be flat in bed when he should be outdoors working. Lucky that Melanie will have him. In this painting, I'm like a Hollywood star."

"You *are* a Hollywood star, Follum. I thought so from the beginning."

"Really?"

"I would choose you as Leif Erickson or the Mountain King or the King of Norway if I were a casting agent on Sunset Boulevard. And if you're the unattractive one, I can't wait to meet your brothers."

Follum had nothing to say, praise like this so rare from his family. We found time for more sittings on the following week-end and on the third Saturday I announced that it was done. By then, most of the enlisted men in the quarters building had made a trip down to Room 318 to inspect the progress, to stand over my shoulder. The yellow background color took another two weeks to fully dry, so the portrait received more attention. Callard wanted me to paint him as a Great Man of History and Parsons, one of my roommates, asked how much I charged.

"What do you think it's worth, Parsons?" I asked.

"Maybe forty dollars?"

"How about fifty?"

I had already agreed to paint Callard for thirty, so things were looking up. I thought that Callard's painting asked to be darker than Follum's and a profile rather than front view. I could visualize him as a Medici Pope, whoever the most evil one was; I tried to remember the Bellini profile with a misty view of Florence in a window beyond, a wicked man overlooking his urban holdings. Could I catch Callard's flickering eyes in a flat painting?

The finished portrait had him in a high collared shirt of deep Italian red, he gazing out the window towards the light, the back of his head shading very dark. The portrait fell into place in two sessions and I was delighted with its elegance. Callard claimed that I was a genius, I had captured his innate sweetness. He would show his bierstube friends in Little Poland that very night, or was it too wet to carry about? He *must* show it and he would be ever so careful, he would not put fingerprints in the fresh surface. However, could he wait to pay me until after payday?

Parsons, I pictured as a Kafka-like governmental official, humorless but just, and I asked him to wear a dark coat and black tie. The canvas came together as easily as Callard's over two days, but I questioned whether or not I had trod too heavily on the bureaucratic look with the leaden gray background, the lighting across the left side of his face as if from a high prison window. Parsons did not look at it during the progress. I told him that it was done and turned it around.

"Oh my goodness, I look like a member of the Komintern, Bradford."

"Maybe I got too severe with the gray browns, too academic, too Soviet."

"It does make me look ruthless. Without friends."

"Stern, I would say, decisive and authoritative."

"The more I look at it, the more I see my father."

"That's not bad, is it?"

"He was the manager of the coal mine in Scranton, really stern."

"I can try another one in warmer colors."

"No. No. This is growing on me and I think my mother will love it. Do you actually see me as this hard hearted, Bradford?"

He talked himself into liking it a lot, and on Monday proudly showed it around the Historical Section. Captain McQuire put her hand across her mouth with the longest look and said that I had definitely caught Parsons's steadfastness. A career in the Diplomatic Corps surely awaited her. Yet something had changed in my art, I knew. I had not studied or practiced since those early portraits, uniformly disliked or ridiculed, but these new portraits pleased both me and the sitters. Did gifts arrive from on high for a painter, unbidden new talents? Why were the gods favoring me now?

As talk went around Schloss Issel about a portrait painter living in the enlisted men's quarters, I received a typewritten note from the colonel's aide-de-camp. Please come by the colonel's office after work tomorrow, signed, Captain Takashima for the Commander. The note paper had a sphinx in the corner and a narrow perimeter band of gold.

I was accompanied by the captain into the colonel's office, his desk ten yards from the door. The colonel asked both of us to sit down. He continued to read for several minutes whatever he was studying when we came in. I looked at his face and thought I could do a fair likeness, but I knew I was heading into more difficult terrain. My friends back on the third floor were not in any way threatening, I could ignore even a hint of displeasure, but this was different, more disquieting.

The colonel looked up from his papers, stacking them neatly. He said, "Specialist Bradford. We've heard good comment about your painting from several of the staff here. Your portraits. You're said to be a talented man."

"Thank you, sir. I've just been sketching small studies of my friends. I want to study art back in the States, get up to professional level."

"You seem to be there already. It's Mrs. Rosscommon who is interested, Bradford. Will you paint her portrait?"

"It's been a long while since I've painted a lady, sir. I don't know." I was lying, because I had never painted a woman.

"I would greatly appreciate it if you would paint Mrs. Rosscommon. She's mentioned it several times to me and I've learned to pay attention to that."

Captain Takashima intervened. "The colonel's car will take you up to the residence and wait to bring you back. Can you be ready for the first sitting by Saturday morning?"

"Yes, sir."

He ushered me out with, "We'll have high expectations, Bradford."

Colonel Rosscommon was the commander of Schloss Issel, from whom all authority flowed, but now I wondered if there was yet a higher ledge where Mrs. Rosscommon lurked, watching her wishes flutter down like plum blossoms. Hadn't Catherine the Great summoned her favorites from the cavalry, finding more and more soldiers for her appetites at ever lower levels? I would much have preferred to paint the colonel himself, a stereotypical crag-jawed old soldier with white hair. Could I deliver whatever it was that Mrs. Rosscommon wanted?

What had started as a joy painting Follum had now turned into a chore. I could picture in my mind a letter, artfully presented in my best cursive script, being opened by blue-veined hands with jeweled fingers, *Mister Bradford Regrets That His Powers Are At Low Tide Today So He Will Be Unable To Sail Off On the Aegean With Mrs. Rosscommon.*

The car arrived at 1000 hours, the driver offering no assistance with the easel or paints. He was the unhelpful same at the residence, a villa on a high hill overlooking Bad Issel and a crescent curve in the Neckar River. A German maid let me in as the car pulled away and parked.

"Mrs. Rosscommon waits for you in the sunroom. This way."

She was looking out over the Neckar River valley from the window with her arms crossed, a thought-out pose, I was sure. The minute I saw her I knew we were in for trouble. The head on the woman was several sizes too small, not just slightly so, but remarkably so. I instantly thought of Henry Walling, a lesser-known signer of the Constitution, who historians described as having the tallest boots in Philadelphia and a head the size of a large apple. Perhaps hers was not quite so small as an apple.

"Hello, Mr. Bradford. Would you like some tea as we talk?" Her neck was long and graceful, however.

"Yes, ma'am."

"I have heard the most wonderful things about your talent."

"Thank you."

The immediate concern was about how to depict her head, slightly larger than it really was, so she looked like other people or as tiny as it was? If it was larger, she would know that I had detected her cruel disproportion and was perhaps mocking her. She would be furious. If as it was, she would see how out of scale she was, like a photograph that shocks people how heavy they have become and she would be equally upset. Maybe if I just painted her head with no shoulders, the dilemma was solved. There would be nothing to relate the startling size of her skull to her body. But she was ahead of me.

"I see a mid-length portrait, Mr. Bradford, shoulders with a suggestion of upper arms. Far enough down to include my pearls, my grandmother's, but not much below. What do you think?"

"We'll give that a try, Mrs. Rosscommon."

When I set up the easel, I sensed a way out. "Mrs. Rosscommon, I've brought only a very small canvas, not enough for a mid-length with pearls without reducing the scale. It's so much better to work exactly life-size, don't you think, and your face and upper neck would fit perfectly on this with plenty of air all around."

Did I hear the ice cracking? She looked at me the longest time and then said yes, of course. This is why wise artists do not want to paint kings and popes, to bring their heavenly torsos into question. I do not think my hand actually quivered as I started the charcoal drawing, but there was a strong quaking in my mind.

She asked, "Are you from the South, Mr. Bradford?"

"Yes, ma'am. My grandmother's favorite uncle was a Confederate hero."

"What surname is that?"

"Merrill. Mifflin Merrill."

We talked about the old South as I worked, she a general's daughter from Alabama. She met the colonel at one of the general's levees. I resisted the urge to ask if there were Wallings or apple orchards in her family. I wondered if anybody in her life had ever mentioned her head, like never talking about an old veteran's limp or ignoring your best friend's stutter. What strange places the personal residences of the high-ranking officers must be. *How was your day on the front, dearie? Not bad, only a few hundred went down in the morning and we had a nice lunch in the tent of those small shrimp from the North Sea. That's good, here's some more tapioca, my love.*

It took two more week-ends to finish the portrait. I grew to like Mrs. Rosscommon in our time together, her graciousness never faltering, and I felt extreme guilt about her head. My painting of her was on a sky-blue ground with a strong morning light across her face. I managed to include the suggestion of her necklace, no shoulders whatsoever, and I was proud of her skin color, quite like an English beauty.

"I love it, Mr. Bradford."

"That's good, ma'am. I worry that something won't be right."

"There is something wrong, however. The colonel says that I am a very vain woman, but I can't help knowing how I look, can I? *Every detail.* Don't worry, what's wrong with the painting is only a matter of scale."

I tried not to show my terror. We were going to talk about the dreaded head? How would I answer this? Was there a small prison under the personal residence, one especially for me and the pastry cooks and the florists that brought displeasure to this hill?

"It's my mouth. You've made it a trifle too small."

"Have I?"

"Grandmother always thought my mouth much too large. This new version is just fine, more lady-like. She would approve highly."

"I could work on it, if you want."

"Let's not enlarge or diminish anything, Mr. Bradford."

# WIGS AND BUCKLES

A heart that loves had better be...
armed for trouble.
— *Emily Dickinson*

WITHOUT ASKING THE PRICE FOR the portrait, Mrs. Rosscommon wrote a check for two hundred dollars, a sum so large I would never have had the nerve to request it. Delighted as I was, I knew a life in portraits did not await me. I had other images in my head, ones that were not faces or the human form. If there were bad aspects to being an artist, the good side was that you did not have to listen to anyone else; you could paint whatever you wanted without a critical eye over your shoulder. Portraits reeked of servitude, your talent as a hostage to the vanity of high position. Come to the house next Thursday, my talented friend, but be sure to enter by the back door, the staff entrance. I would not set myself up to hear that there is a little something wrong with the mouth, Bradford, please work harder. To be an artist meant to be free, paint the canvases you wanted, no proctor looking over your shoulder. Or so I thought at the time.

My emotional response to being so far from Middleton, away from Henry Zilbert, my mother and father and everyone stateside, was to blot them out, take up with zest this new life in a new land. I was excited about Europe and its mysteries, but I knew that I was at heart the product of the New World, and particularly a son of the unschooled stretches of West Texas. Even if I succeeded in Europe, I would always be known as that Harold Bradford, he's from the American West. A foreigner, you know.

I spent the weekend before Christmas writing cards to the people who kept coming up into my consciousness, not letting me go. I had a dream that their faces were beginning to fade, replaced by a court dance where Follum, Callard and Captain McQuire, hand-in-hand, in white wigs and buckled shoes, danced a gavotte in the middle of my Middleton family and friends, who fearfully lined the edges of the parquet floor in home-spun clothes with muddy work shoes. The Old World was winning as the wigs bowed low at music's end, arms spread wide.

The front side of my Christmas cards, from a stack in the village shop, was a vintage Baedeker photograph of Schloss Issel in the snow, the grape-vines covered with long rows of white and a flock of birds flying in the sky above. An squarish automobile was moving, out of focus, on the street below. I drew an arrow pointing out "My Room." Only a few lines could be written on the inside page.

*"Dear Henry: I've missed you a lot, bud, and wish we were going through this experience together. So many new people and ideas, I won't even start, but in sixteen months I will be back with you in Middleton. Can we take up the plan to share the house on Water Street? I hope so, then we can spend a lot of Merry Christmases together. Your friend, Harold."*

I immediately wanted to rewrite the card, to tell Henry that I should have lied to the draft board, claimed some fake family illness, stayed on in Middleton and that I loved him. Our time in the Water Street house would be too precious to give up, even if deserting the army life was the only way. Somehow, I could not simply tell him.

*"Dear Mother: I hate the way we left it with you mad at me. I understand that I did not live up to your expectations, but this is only the first act of our life together. You will be pleased that I think I may be growing up, because I noticed my socks are showing more under my trousers. Or maybe it's just the laundry-water here is too hot. Merry Christmas, Mother. Love, H."*

*"Dear Father: We never could talk about anything important and I now believe that won't change. I realize you have tried to connect as best you could. It was me who shut my ear-lids, which even now are only barely opened. The other night while I was walking in a snowstorm down to Bad Issel, I imagined that I heard you calling my name without choking. What did you want to say to me? Merry Christmas, Dad. Love, H."*

I reread my card to father and wondered if I should write it again with the bland endearments of the past. No, it was better to speak the truth. Too much that was unspoken needed now to have the substance of words.

*"Dear Jim: I left you with the parents bent all out of shape about me and I apologize. But you are the blessed son that they really wanted and loved, so it won't be hard for you. If the past years have been awkward, I see a clear space coming, the sunny uplands as the English say, where we'll be the brothers we ought to be. Love, Harold."*

*"Dear Luanna: It's your first anniversary as Mrs. Jerome Bentham and I trust that marriage is everything you expected. I was hurt when you said yes to someone else without a word to me. I know now what an unsatisfactory husband I would have been and how right your mother, the stylish Anne Lu, was in disliking me. Get out of Middleton and away from my Lulu,, she told me with a snarl. How does the outspoken Anne Lu get on with your Jerry, by the way? Have some nice holidays. H."*

*"Dear Miss Lender: Since you were my favorite teacher, I don't understand why I never got around to telling you so. Who would have thought that Senior English could be the best course I ever took, bar none, all those university hours included? I'm in Germany now, a draftee, and wanted you to know that I'm going to art school when I return. You suggested it so many years ago; why didn't I listen? May I come by and talk when I get back? Harold Bradford."*

*"Dear Mrs. Flack: I am sorry that I was such a twerp. You looked so patriotic and brave, at attention when we left for Arkansas. The Draft Board is a hard civic duty, when I know you would rather be at home cooking chess pies and scrubbing the walls around the oven with Lysol. Let's hope that the draftees who come after me are more pliant and appreciative. Merry Christmas. Harold Bradford."*

I posted all the envelopes with eagle Air Mail stamps, but the mail room clerk told me that there was only a slim chance that they would get home by New Years, well too late for Christmas. I thought it was symbolic of my life before now, that my love, appreciation or attempts at ridicule arrived several days too late, well after the main event.

The Bierstube Langenscheidt was full that night, mostly with the men from the Schloss Issel. I wondered if their thoughts like mine had turned to home-town friends and families, lives they had left behind. Follum was there ahead of me.

He said, "I got some Christmas cards off last week. My family and Melanie. I haven't heard what she thinks of the portrait yet."

I said, "She'll probably hate it."

"No, she'll see that the artist thought I was more handsome than I really am."

"I paint what I see in front of me."

"I think Melanie will be jealous, thinking that you have become too close a friend, better than she and I ever were."

"That is good, not bad, Eric. To have a new friend."

Her responding letter arrived just after Christmas day and Eric let me read it. It was written with a forward slant in purple ink on lavender paper, each "i" dotted with a circle.

*"Dear Eric: I don't know what to say about your portrait. Your family looked at it for the longest time before your older brother told me that it said Vanity, not a good quality for a future Lutheran music director. I was surprised how attractively Bradford pictured you, as if he saw hidden qualities that we did not. I told your mother that I was worried that Bradford depicted a man who might turn worldly in Europe and not return to White Cloud for many years. I hope I'm wrong, my dear. Melanie."*

Eric looked guilty as he said, "Sometimes Melanie worries too much."

"She seems to have noticed something odd about your portrait. If for nothing else, I'm glad it made everyone at home take notice of you."

"I can hear them talking about it around the Sunday table."

"Good."

New Years Day passed before I got a reply to any of my own letters. I began to think that in writing them I had been too much of a smart-ass. I could hear Luanna telling me to stop putting a barb into everything that I said, to say it nicely and stop talking.

It would not surprise me if no one answered, but on 3 January I got a letter. It was from my mother, six pages on both sides of her large handwriting, space for only a few lines per page.

*"Dear Boy: I also felt unhappy when you left, and I am relieved that you are growing up. You were a very bad baby, a good boy, then bad again as a college student, so the mere cycles of life say better times ahead. Your father has been under the weather and your brother says he misses you.*

*I'm sure you've heard that your Luanna found her Jerry in bed with the garden-man last summer. Everyone chattered for weeks. Luanna's family had already finalized a trust fund for Jerry, so he kept both the money and the Mexican. Anne Lu hasn't played bridge for months.*

*On the rebound, Luanna married your friend Henry Zilbert. They are leaving college to honeymoon in the old Zilbert house. We all love you here, Harold, so come home safely. Your loving mother.*

*PS: Three Evening Grosbeaks in the backyard yesterday."*

So I should not expect an answer from either Henry or Luanna, one way or another. I was not happy that the Zilbert house would be unavailable for our bachelor parties and did not want to think too closely about Henry making love to Luanna. It pleased me, however, that Anne Lu was having an unpleasant time.

I realized that Henry Zilbert had let me love him, allowed my adoration, but it was available only if I stayed with him, amused him and distracted him from the offers of others. His love would move on if I failed to keep the golden balls up in the air. King Henry needed a Fool to fill the long Middleton afternoons, to admire him, adore him. I had adored him.

My father and my brother did not write, nor did Mrs. Flack, so I was happy to see my English teacher's firm handwriting on the second letter, arriving 10 January.

*"Dearest Harold: I am heartened that you are going to art school. You will, I am sure, make a good life as a painter. I was reading the letters of Matisse this last week and came across this: 'Art was the lover that loved me the most. Amelie was afraid of me, my children did not understand, the critics disliked me and my friends were either confused or envious. When those I ought to depend upon faltered, I always took up a brush and painted the first line, exactly plumb in the center from top to bottom of the canvas. Life would be getting better, I knew.'*

*Please do come by when you are in Middleton and maybe we can figure out how you can draw that first plumb line. Fondly, Anette Lender."*

A few weeks later, I received a third letter, this one an unexpected answer from once divorced and twice married Luanna. It was typed neatly on thick gray stationery with a deeper gray border with the single initial "Z." She wrote,

*"Dear Harold: I should not feel a shred of guilt for marrying Henry, but I do. I could have told you face-to-face, I suppose. Mother and I have talked a great deal about you and believe you are incapable of love, a cripple. To ask you to return the affection that I so openly offered would be like asking a fish to fly or a bird to swim. You could not help it. We feel sorry for you, forgive you. LZ."*

Her letter did not cheer up a German afternoon, especially the "LZ" bit at the end. And what about the pelicans and ducks that can swim, and the Barbados fish that can fly, anyway? As I walked over to the Bierstube Langenscheidt I realized that Luanna had reported nothing about Jerry and the gardener's peppery time in the sack or the missing millions that gave Anne Lu such sick headaches, but I thought I had learned what a bittersweet smile was. I, the bird that could not swim, had one on as I walked into the smoky front room, replete with brewery aromas and the acrid smell of Germans four nights away from a bath. I doubted that the beer-drinkers would notice either my damp feathers or my astringent smile, both honestly earned.

# Horst und Wolfgang

Our lives are Swiss –
So still – so cool –
Till some odd afternoon
The Alps neglect their curtains
— *Emily Dickinson*

GREGORY PARSONS CAME FROM Scranton, Pennsylvania and was headed to law school when the draft threatened to pull him into the infantry. Although it was manly and brave to join the infantry, many young men held a horror of the front line with a rifle, even a repeating rifle. If he enlisted in the Army before his call for the draft, Parsons could choose whatever branch of the service he preferred. He enlisted and was promised a space as a Counterintelligence Agent, exciting work in the field. For this added luster, he must spend three years in the service, instead of the draftee's two.

However, the Army did not keep its word and assigned him the analyst desk next to me in the Historical Section. He complained, officially with letters up the chain of command, and unofficially to everyone within earshot. No one came to his aid.

Time had eventually lessened his plaint and now he was at the end of his second year as an analyst, only one more year to go.

Late one week in the Historical Section, Captain McQuire sat on the corner of my desk and with her glasses in hand motioned Parsons to come near. She leaned down in a conspiratorial stance.

"High command has asked us to prepare a short overview of the politics of the German Republic as they are today in nineteen fifty-seven. No more than ten pages, how the government works, personalities, political parties, the issues involved and our comments on everything. It will be a Confidential document, sent to the commanders of all outfits in European Command in their daily briefing. Apparently very little is known in the units."

"Only ten pages for all that?" I asked.

"More and it won't be read. Five would be better. Can you put that together by the middle of next week? No Secret or Top Secret matter included."

Parsons said, "Yes, Captain."

She said, "The two of you work out who will do what. I'll check on you in a day or two."

We conferred after she left. Parsons would research the personalities, quote the sources, and I would write the outline of the government, history of problems and the issues involved. It was a welcome change from the dossiers that we faced every day at the Historical Section.

Parsons left for the Central Registry while I pulled together the documents I needed: *World Politics* by Walter Lippman, *Germany Today*, *World Almanacs* and *Political Geography of the Cold War*. The new government at Bonn was only just being empowered, the occupation relinquishing their powers slowly. Despite the wishes of the Allies, the Social Democrats were gaining as much power as Adenauer's Christian Democrats. The coalition majority was as loosely stitched together as the future, I wrote, savoring the telling phrases that would illuminate an entire army.

By working over the weekend, I had my five pages written, leaving five for Parsons to insert the personalities involved. We interleaved the two types of information together and I typed up the finished document. We had a sense of self-importance, policy makers at work, as we presented the Captain with the finished text.

She read the pages while we stood at her desk.

"This is first-rate."

"Thanks, ma'am."

"I'll touch it up here and there, pass it along to high command. Why don't you both take the rest of the week off? You deserve a three-day pass."

That's how Parsons and I earned our trip to Switzerland. Normally, I would choose Follum and Callard as companions, and Parsons had travel chums of his own. I viewed a trip with Parsons better than time in Bad Issel, and he must have done the same. It was an easy drive, Parsons offering to take us south in his new Volkswagen bug.

Snow was on the mountains, with patches of mist rising from the lake when we arrived in Lucerne, clear and cold. Parsons found a place to park and we asked in a lakeside bierstube if they had rooms available. Yes, upstairs, with a breakfast included. After we took our cases up, we walked around the lake front, exploring the streets along the river that led away from the lake, lined with shops, offices and restaurants. It had become dark when we chose a place to have dinner, and, afterwards, we walked back to our bierstube for a nightcap.

It was a pine-paneled room, full of smoke and beer-drinkers. All of the customers were men, not a particularly unusual arrangement for drinking establishments in Germany and Switzerland. Perhaps the Swiss did not stare at Americans quite as intently as the Germans. Two young men at a far table, twins it seemed, looked our way without a breather.

Parsons noticed them, and asked, "Should we send them a beer?"

"That would be nice, let's do."

"I had hoped we would see some girls to send a drink."

I asked, "So why send the men a drink instead?"

"They seemed friendly, smiling. Many aren't here in Europe."

"You're right. I expect they'll come over to thank us."

The two men waved at us and smiled when their beers were delivered. They did not come immediately over to talk. After we had several more beers ourselves, Parson went to the WC. One of the brothers came right over and took Parson's seat.

He said, "You and your friend are together?"

"Yes, we're friends."

"That's all, friends?"

I nodded yes.

"Then, you're on your own?"

"More or less."

"Will you go to bed with me and my brother?"

"I don't know." Who would have thought the Swiss were so bold?

"Where are you staying?"

"Right here in a room over the bierstube."

"Come outside to the streetlight after your friend goes to sleep. We'll wait for you."

"I'm not sure. What's your name?"

"Horst. My brother is Wolfgang. What part of the States are you from?"

"Texas. West Texas."

"Then it's settled. Wolfgang has always wanted to be with a Texas cowboy, to give him joy."

"I'm not a cowboy."

"Just coming from Texas is good enough. We are very good, the best in Lucerne. Everybody says so."

"I believe you. It will be after midnight if I can meet you."

"What's your name?"

"Bradford. And here is my friend, Gregory Parsons."

Horst shook his hand with vigor, and then returned to the table with his brother. Parsons asked what he said. I told him that they wanted say thanks and find out where we were from.

He said, "They seem like nice fellows. Maybe we can make friends with them."

Just as I said good idea, the brothers got up to go. They came by the table and said Good Night, West Texas and Gregory. I saw that they were truly identical, short-statured, blond, blue-eyed and they both moved like athletes. Weight-lifting and shot-put, close to the ground sports, rather than sprint-runners. Parsons shook their hands and the men departed.

We walked around the middle of the city for a half hour, I thinking I could see the brothers in the shadows behind us, but it was only a false movement, a gust of wind moving a branch whenever I looked closer. Parsons saw nothing behind him and very little in front if he was talking. I wondered what they taught the field agents in Baltimore for them to be so unaware of their surroundings.

He said, "Well, I need to turn in."

"Do you want one more beer, on the way back?"

"I've had enough. You go, though."

"No, I need to go to bed, too."

Well past midnight, I heard Parson's steady breathing under the pillow that he had put over his head. I tried to summon good sense and renunciation. This would be a stupid thing to do, cavorting late at night with two unknown men, however attractive they might be.

I dressed quietly, walked out and down to the street. It was empty. I went over to the street light and waited a bit, my breath making clouds in the air. In five minutes Horst appeared in the doorway opposite; he walked over to me.

"We have rooms right upstairs. Did your friend not want to come?"

"No, he's more interested in women."

"He seemed to have the eye for us, as well."

"Take it from me, he only likes women."

I followed Horst up the stairway, the building hot and steamy from being closed. Wolfgang opened the door and it was even hotter in their room. He immediately came towards me and put his hands on either side of my face. They were warm on my winter-cooled skin.

Wolfgang unbuttoned my shirt and Horst unbuckled the belt, pulling it out of the trouser loops. These were professional hands, accustomed to giving joy to another man. I kissed each one in turn and they lifted me up like a pharaoh in a sedan chair. After placing me gently on their rumpled bed, they moved their bodies across mine with slow expertise, acting in unison for a while then taking different parts of me to explore.

Horst may have spoken the better English, but Wolfgang made the better love. Odd that Wolfgang's touch was so electric, while Horst's was not. How could identical twins be so different? When I returned their love, took the active role, they became recipients for whatever I tried. Minutes stretched out into an hour or so, until I had no more love to give.

Horst asked, "Why don't you wait until it is light? We can have love all over again."

"No, I need to get back."

"Will you come again to Lucerne?"

"Maybe. In the spring."

"Then, all three of us are happy again. Wolfgang makes love to you, you make love to me."

"Is that how you always do it?"

"No, sometimes other ways."

"Do you ever make love to each other?"

"No. We choose a man like you." He put his hand flat on my chest.

"What do you think of when I am kissing Wolfgang?"

"We are the same person. You are kissing me, too."

As if I were a small child, the two men helped me get dressed again, pulling up my trousers, slipping on socks and tying the shoes on my feet, gently buttoning my shirt, kissing my skin as they went. As I thought about when I might be able to return, a long week-end, and how long the train trip might be, Horst said, "Why not come back and live with us for a while? You can stay here while we go to work, then we come home and cover you with pleasure. We make a good triad."

"I'm in the US Army. I can't come back and live with you."

"We make much better love than the Army does."

"I know. This is the first time in Europe that I have made such love."

"You are a very funny man," he said.

"No, it's true."

"Yes, yes, say goodnight to our first-timer, Wolfgang."

"Good night, West Texas."

I walked back across the cold street to the bierstube, the key to the room opening the staircase door and up to Parsons, who was still exuding a small snore from under his comforter. I felt happy as I went to sleep, that I had found a part of me that was lost. If I had been bolder back then, could I have made this happen with Henry Zilbert, made him mine instead of Luanna's? I could see his long legs, his languid sexiness, as my tiredness gave in to sleep.

The stube served us a small breakfast down in the bar: brotchen, butter, marmalade, coffee and juice. I was wondering what to say to Parsons.

He said, "Did you see the brothers again when you went out?"

"Yes. I couldn't sleep. I thought you didn't hear me."

"No, I heard you going out. It's okay, Bradford. I knew you wanted some more to drink but I can't take in as much as you."

"We did have a few more. Since it was after hours, we went right across the street at their place. They told me how hard it is to make a living in Switzerland now. They both work at construction, one a carpenter, the other a mason."

"What are their names?"

"Wolfgang and Horst."

"Maybe we should come back here in the summer, take them on a trip. It's nice to have Swiss friends."

I admired Parsons for his trusting, unquestioning nature. After breakfast, we had the whole morning in Lucerne to walk around, see the city center and the museums before the drive back. There was an exhibit at the museum of a Swiss painter, sensual paintings of abstracted bodies across each other. Men's legs spread over a woman's leg, or genderless bodies together in angular designs, the heads and feet off the canvas. Sensitive to the idea that more than two people can come together for sex, I counted six legs in one painting, eight entwined in another.

These were large paintings with the actual body parts stylized. I told Parsons that I really liked the paintings.

He said, "I don't see the attraction."

"They're so sexual, Parsons."

"They are?"

"Look here and here and here."

"Legs and arms don't get my willy up, Bradford."

As we drove north back to Germany, I offered a time at the wheel. I wondered if all the Swiss dreamed of making love with three people together, or even more

Was I extra-susceptible to sexual suggestion because of the night's escapade, like having a sun-burn from too long at the beach? How amusing that sex blossomed so well behind the chalet facades with window boxes and red-checkered curtains. Who would have thought that Lucerne, city of cream, butter and wooden clocks, was the sexual epicenter of Europe?

We came into the outskirts of Stuttgart and the new snow made the autobahn slippery. While the Volkswagen struggled up the exit for Schloss Issel, I asked Parsons if he had a good time.

"I was just thinking about it. Weather would be nicer there if we went back in the summer."

"Would you want to go to Lucerne again?"

"You bet. Maybe McQuire will have another project for us soon, politics of France or the government of Belgium. Another three-day pass with a week-end. We could take Manfred and Wolfgang down to Lake Como. Find some Italian girls. I hear that they like Americans. We could drink lots of red wine, instead of beer."

"*Horst* and Wolfgang."

"Oh, right. Nice fellows, though."

# Light Lunch in Möblingen

O Captain! my Captain! our fearful trip is done.
— *Walt Whitman*

CAPTAIN MCQUIRE WAS DONE up as a gypsy dancer, a full velvet skirt, black high-heeled pumps with ankle straps, the classic peasant blouse, circle ear-rings and a black wig. She was a tall woman anyway, but in this outfit she brushed the stratosphere, a giant, strong-willed gypsy of the likes seldom seen in West Germany.

"Disguises, Bradford. The key to successful intelligence work," she said as she climbed easily beside me in the cab of the truck. Follum was in the driver's seat, I in the middle and McQuire on the right passenger seat. With her elbow on the window sill, she jangled her bracelets as we turned to inspect her.

"Yes, ma'am."

She continued, "I've slipped through tight spaces in my covert attire. Istanbul. Oslo. Even Berlin."

"This one is especially good, ma'am. The pattern-on-pattern works."

"Don't push it, Bradford. I almost chose Callard for this exercise, instead."

Follum and I had been ordered to dress as bakers, complete with a hair dusting of flour back in the supply room. Verisimilitude, the captain said. We wore white two-piece coveralls with an embroidered motto on our shirt pockets and on the brim of our caps. *Brot Ist Leben* it read, but I doubted that anybody would be fooled. We were sitting in the cab of a large delivery van with more bakery wording along the sides and back.

This was the day for the practice evacuation of the Bad Issel Counterintelligence Headquarters, by regulation an annual event but in reality only every third year or so. It was the scenario of what would happen if the Russians invaded from the East. Considering the filing cabinets full of secrets, our offices were presumed to be the prime target for the battalions of Russian tanks racing west. With only a ten-hour head start, we were ordered, in an actual invasion, to load up the two hundred cabinets with the most sensitive files into the fake bread delivery trucks and other vehicles disguised as florist trucks, ice delivery vans and the like. The remaining files were to be set afire with the timed magnesium grenades which were affixed to every cabinet.

As headquarters burned like Manderly, we were to flee with the most secret of secret papers to Switzerland as headquarters burned, through Zurich down to Geneva, across the South of France, eventually to Lisbon, where ships awaited to take us and the documents stateside. This year's exercise was entitled Operation Summer Picnic, but in our briefing for the long day, McQuire cut through the laughing and gossiping.

No files were actually loaded up on this practice evacuation, as we were merely rehearsing the path to the sea and safety. Back in the truck, Captain McQuire said, "Let's get under way, Follum. I have the map in this reticule."

"May I see it, ma'am?"

"Need to know, Follum. The less you know, the less you tell. I'll direct you."

Follum was not familiar with the operation of a German commercial vehicle, so we lurched forward, then backward while he searched for the reverse gear. He was quick with motors and machines, however, and we were out the front gate in a few minutes. I thought we ought to take the autobahn as far south as we could, then veer off to Zurich on a major country road. With the certainty of Russian torture if we were overtaken, speed was paramount.

"Side roads are the essence of stealth, men. We'll slither by the dark farmlands and unsuspecting villages. Lisbon by Friday at the latest."

McQuire could see in her mind the grand sweep of the exercise, democratic secrecy fleeing the certain cruelty of dictators. Like the retreat from Dunkirk, this was a vital chess move in the game of freedom. Follum and I both knew that it would be called off before lunchtime, as it always was, and each team given a score on how far from headquarters they had come. Ours was the team from the Historical Section, our captain on the point.

It was dark and misty when we reached the suburbs of Stuttgart, past the Daimler-Benz factories and then out along open fields of cabbage and sugar beets. The Swiss border was somewhere ahead of us in the fog.

At the briefing last night, we had been told that each truck was on its own, no convoys for the enemy to spot from the air. If the MIG rockets destroyed a few of us, some were sure to get through. Callard had asked what *our* Air Force was doing in this whole matter, but McQuire told him to stop questioning authority. Nose down to your own assignment. Each soldier like a stitch in the Army's blanket. I thought that a surprisingly womanly metaphor from our captain.

We drove through the first village and the lights were

coming on in the houses. Several farm tractors were already on the streets, each with a wooden wagon behind.

"Pass them, Follum. But carefully."

Follum lightly honked his horn and the first tractor in the queue pulled to the far right side of the road, letting us pass, but only after the farmer raised his fist at the interlopers. McQuire rolled down her window and called out *Veilen dank, mein freund* to the mystified farmer. As the fog lifted, we drove out into the fields again. Follum unrolled his window, too, and the spring country air filled the truck's cabin, a fecund, wet smell of grass and animals. Somewhere between raw sewage and newly mown hay.

I knew that Follum, from the many trips we had taken together, loved that smell. It reminded him of home and the Wisconsin family farm. I, being the tender product of privilege, found it redolent of offal and urine, smelly beyond belief.

"Pew," I said.

McQuire scowled at me and asked, "Follum, aren't *you* a farm boy?"

"Yes, Captain."

"My fondest childhood memories are of my grandparent's farm in Kansas. Corn standing high and waving wheat, just outside of McPherson. Roast chicken and White Queen corn on the cob. Are you going back to be one of our nation's farmers?"

"No, ma'am. I was studying to be a music director. Church music."

"Good German peasant music. Almost as good as farm life."

I stepped in to tell about Follum. "Ma'am, Follum was on a full scholarship at St. Olaf University, an honors student, but he dropped out for a semester to help out at home. The draft board got him, otherwise he would now be doing his graduate work."

McQuire asked, "Why did you get drafted, Bradford?"

"The draft board caught me because I flunked out."

McQuire said, "You're not a dumbo; just bored, I suspect. I like you draftees for my courier work; I feel a bonding there. You boys pick up things quicker, respond with imagination in the field. Regular Army agents are brave but slow on the uptake, generally dim. Too much testosterone, scratching their balls when I talk to them. Give me inductees, any old time." She was clearly trying to bond with the two Selective Service boys she had at hand.

I said, "Maybe the years of squirming away from the draft boards, scurrying this way and that, have imbued us with a wariness. An ability to see things that the average soldier can't."

"Could be, Bradford. Are you naturally wary now?"

"I think so. Germany today is so filled with people that wish us harm. Every week I see people down in Bad Issel with binoculars looking up at our windows, men following us onto the *Strassenbahns*, other men taking up the tail downtown when we cross the street, and there are those women who wait on corners for us to pass. They know our faces."

"Those women pose other dangers. Are you susceptible to the *frauleins*, Bradford?"

"No."

"I thought not. What about you, Follum?"

"No, as well, Captain."

"Good. Upper staff thinks most of them to be enemy agents, and the ones with the lowest blouses are most surely in Soviet employ. They'll ply you with schnapps and beer and drinking songs, bed you, and suck away your secrets."

"Suck, ma'am?"

"Only a turn of phrase. Keep your eyes on the road, Follum."

We were coming into Möblingen, a narrow road between twenty stone cottages with dark tiled roofs. The villagers were awake now, men already departed on tractors for the fields, women swatting the comforters with Malacca hoops and hanging the rugs to air in the windows, gossiping from window to window. Bakers in trucks must be German, so they waved. At the far side of town the truck lurched to a stop and the three of us looked at a large blinking red light on the dashboard.

"What does that mean, Follum?" McQuire asked.

"I don't know. Perhaps overheating. I can barely read the letters under it."

I said, "What does *Sich ausleeren* mean, Captain?"

"No technical Deutsch in my training, but I think it means empty. How did this happen?"

Follum nudged me with his arm. We had earlier that morning heard the Motor Pool's assessment of the captain. Sergeant McCoy said, "So the two of you are Queenie's new driver and shot gun? Have a good time, boys." We had been set up with a near-empty truck. Best not to let Queenie know, however.

McQuire said, "I'll get out and hitch a ride to the nearest gas station. I have a phrase book here. Let me see... *Wo ist der abschliessen benzinplatz?*"

I said, "Perfect accent, ma'am, but I think I should go."

"Nonsense. An attractive woman always gets more rides than a mere baker."

"Perhaps, so. But there might be danger. A woman on her own."

"Recall, Bradford, who instructs your ju-jitsu class."

"You're right, Captain. Besides, I didn't bring any German money."

"Money? Oh, rats."

Follum said, "Maybe you can just borrow some gas."

She said, "Doubtful, but I'll figure it out."

The three of us pushed the disabled truck off onto the grassy bank. The captain re-arranged her skirt, tucked in the escaping corners of the embroidered blouse and flounced the thick strands of her wig. In the full light of day, the captain's gypsy regalia looked tawdry, her wig too chemically black and rope-like. This was going to be a long day, I thought, as I felt a surge of sympathy for the captain and her task.

She did not put out her thumb but waved at the sound of a car approaching. Bracelets jangled. To our surprise, the car stopped and the man leaned over to open the passenger side door with a smile. Or was it a leer?

As she headed his way, I said, "Something on your tooth, Captain," pointing to my left incisor. She rubbed her kerchief on her own tooth as she sauntered over to the stranger.

A feminine rigor took over the captain, her tall frame oddly sinuous as she walked and slid into the seat, closing the door with one graceful pull. While the car drove away, we could see through its rear window the two talking and nodding with their faces turned toward each other. The captain was leaning heavily on the popularity of tall Gypsy women in this Swabian countryside.

There was a small fountain in the middle of Möblingen, so I walked over and washed the flour out of my hair. At first it made a sort of pie dough, but with enough rinsing it came clean. Afterwards, the fountain had long white strings floating about, which took a minute or two to clear out. The housewives watched without comment from their comforter-laden windows, perhaps now suspecting that I was not really a German baker. It would not do to leave their fountain sullied.

Follum's years with the hurry-and-wait of the family harvest told him that this was a good time for a long nap. He rolled up the white jacket part of our uniform and pillowed his head. It annoyed me how easily he could sleep. It would be hours of worry for me.

Food, as well as money, was not on the list of things officially provided in this exercise and as it was well past noon, my stomach rumbled. I doubted that the women in the windows of the village would be offering bread and cheese, now that they knew our real identity. I circled around the truck a few times while Follum continued to nap.

At two in the afternoon, the sedan with the leering man pulled up in front of us with the captain beside him. He was not smiling now. As she got smartly out of the passenger side, her military bearing erased the womanly demeanor of her departure. The trunk opened itself without the man leaving his steering wheel and the captain retrieved a gas container, slamming the door to the trunk. The driver turned around sharply and was off in the direction he had come. Follum took only seconds to empty the can into the truck's gas tank.

I asked, "Was he nice, Captain? Did it go well?"

"Can it, Bradford. Let's go."

"Where to, ma'am?" Follum asked.

"Back to Bad Issel. The exercise was called off at noon. I telephoned from the gas station to verify that and to give them our location." She climbed into the truck and we were off.

I said, "How far did we get, Captain?"

"Not far enough."

"About forty kilometers, I think," Follum said.

She said, "If the hammer had really gone down, we would be in Russian hands by now. Backs being broken on their mobile torture racks, I would guess. Tibetan Prayer Wheels, they're called."

Her wig was entirely gone, her head wrapped with panache in the multi-colored scarf that had been around her neck. As she looked closely at both of us, I knew it was death if I smiled. I looked straight ahead, but I could see that Follum's mouth quivered then stayed resolutely shut. I thought her reticule with the map was missing, as well.

I kept my imagination in check, daring not to think about what it took to get that can of gas. We returned to Bad Issel in silence while I thought about the sound of the wooden gears turning and bones breaking on the mobile racks. These were only the small portable ones, not the console versions back in Moscow. Secrets would pour out of us like birdsong.

McQuire pulled herself together as the headquarters building came into sight. We stopped at the officers' quarters and she stepped down. She pulled off her head-scarf and said, "You men have done very well. I will commend you in my report, details of which should remain strictly *entre nous*." As she walked away, I knew that Callard was waiting to quiz Follum closely about our day. Even if nations were brought low, Follum would not lie and Callard was adept at worming information out of an unwilling subject. The whole headquarters would know by morning.

At the Motor Pool where we left the bakery van, Sergeant McCoy and his gang lingered with smiles at the open doors. The news had made in there already. *Did Queenie and the boys stop in Möblingen for a light lunch? Some fried schnitzel with lemon wedges and a chilled Gewürztraminer?*

The next day at the Historical Section, after returning our disguises to the Supply Room, we could see from our desks into the windows of the adjoining conference room. Draperies were pulled open and the officers from the sections presented their reports, which we could not hear. A large map delineated how far each team evacuated and the section-head in turn stood to present his version of the mock evacuation. The Historical Section marker had the shortest string back to Stuttgart, others were deep into Switzerland, including the highly competitive team from Counterespionage Section. Most clustered just outside of Geneva.

We could see the captain with her hand on the "H" marker, answering many questions and her body language told it all. Worst section, least amount of distance traveled, the nation's secrets in the hand of the enemy, disgrace, disgrace.

The meeting broke up and the Section heads departed. The captain returned to her desk. She looked over at Callard, who was intently studying the middle pages of a thick dossier. She said, "Did I hear a snigger, Callard?"

"No, Captain."

"Splendid. Sniggers could be very dangerous to all concerned."

# THE CLEAR AIR OF WEST TEXAS

> Any man who goes to a psychiatrist
> should have his head examined.
> — *Sam Goldwyn*

WOMEN IN THE ARMY OF 1957 were not given much authority, but McQuire had earned her position in the man's world. The other officers said she was a good leader, great with the men. A key to this may have been her schedule of interviews in her corner office, learning the life details of the staff she depended upon. Interviews took up the first hour of every morning, individual sessions usually no longer than ten minutes, so she got around to everybody in the section in two weeks. Once done, she started the whole process over. Personal problems did not have a long time to fester without her input.

It was my turn again. She had my file open in front of her. "Bradford, sit down. Tell me about West Texas. Do you have a sweetie waiting there?"

"Not any more. We split before I was drafted."

"Did you love her?"

"I guess not enough. She got married without inviting me, divorced him, then married someone else."

"There will be others, I can assure you. What about the best friend that you mentioned last time?"

Captain McQuire's office at the Historical Section was nothing more than a corner that had been windowed off from the main hall with the same casement windows used elsewhere at the Schloss. She could see all fifty desks without turning her head. Callard said that the captain could sense when dossier pages were not turning fast enough and would come out to explore like a sand-crab checking out a curious noise or a shift in the wind.

Nothing about her office was feminine: a perpetual calendar in Khaki-brown, a gray-and-blue Hofbrauhaus mug for pens and pencils, photos of various graduation ceremonies, a black leather desk chair on wheels, a small bookcase with foreign-language dictionaries and city directories. There were two leather-covered side chairs in front of her desk.

In the earlier interviews, I had learned that McQuire wanted exact details about my life, as if she was describing my distinctive symptoms for an academic journal. I was reticent at first, but it had become like an expected trip to the analyst, the doctor ready to commiserate with every revelation. She listened well. We had already talked about my art aspirations, the inability to talk to my father, my mother's sharp tongue and my own sense of drifting.

I answered her question about my best friend. "Henry Zilbert is his name. He's probably riding out to the south pond, shooting dove."

I felt detailed information about Henry and Luanna together was too new to share, like sensitive scar-tissue.

"Is he the one who taught you how to zero-in a rifle?"

"Yes, ma'am. And the Model Twelve Winchester twenty-gauge. Plenty of birds on the Zilbert land at the end of the year, when the grasses dry."

"How do you feel about hunting bigger animals? Deer, elk and bear?"

"I don't like it any more, somehow. And I think I'll quit the dove and quail when I get back. Killing things in the countryside does not seem as much fun as when I was younger."

"I see here your scores at the ranges in Arkansas and Maryland. Very impressive. I never brag, but yours are only very slightly less than mine, well above any average."

"I saw your Expert's Badge on the first day."

"I thought so. Would you be willing to back me up on missions?"

"Missions?"

"Usually very harmless sorties: bringing in suspects, traffic control. Top Secret agendas, so again you would qualify. It's amazing how many of our career field agents are poor shots, like helpless schoolchildren when they look down a sight. Some even shut their eyes as they squeeze the trigger." She shut one eye as if sighting down a barrel.

"You do know that I'm only an analyst, not a field agent?"

"That's just a technicality. I like to have my Sharp-Shooters around me, like watchful, suspicious ladies-in-waiting. The best always have a place with me in the field."

"I'm not so sure that I'm the best, ma'am." And I was solidly sure that I did not want to become a gun-belted lady-in-waiting, much as I admired the captain.

She said, "Let's try you out, sometime. Trial by fire. It says here that you are qualified on the Sub-Machine Gun, as well."

"I really don't mind working at my desk, like the other analysts."

"You were quick-witted and light on your feet on the Zurich trip, Bradford. I'm a good judge of character. There's no specific operation that I have in mind, but I keep my list up to date, just in case. We're known as the Wrecking Squad."

"I guess I would like to be included."

"Nothing dangerous, no soft targets. Patrick in the Mailroom is the liquid expert, a Kansas farm boy, by the way, with another group entirely. I'll set you up for a familiarization weekend with the Beretta rifle, our weapon of choice."

I had no idea what she was talking about. Patrick appeared entirely harmless, sorting letters into the soldiers' boxes. What in the world was a liquid expert?

She asked, "Where is this Zilbert now?"

"He's married and living in the house on Water Street."

"The two of you should have enlisted on the buddy system, hometown friends sharing an assignment next to each other. Then the Army guarantees to keep you together, through thick and thin."

"I wish we could have." Interesting thought: having the Army keep Henry and me together through the rough patches. *No Luanna, you can't have him, Army Rules say hands off.*

McQuire said, "You'll be back there in no time."

"Fifteen more months, Captain."

"Well, then." The interview was over. I suspected that I was meant to feel proud to be on one of McQuire's lists, but this one for the Wrecking Squad portended darker undertakings. Courier duty seemed like pussy-cat work now that firearms and sharp-shooting had entered the equation.

Did McQuire have another, entirely different life and career other than the hum-drum of the Historical Section's great book? Did everybody at Schloss Issel have a cover job, the daily grind, and the real one, more ominous, blacker, more demanding? Mousey desk jobs in the light of day, changing to black karate pajamas and assassinations after the sun set? I thought of the old Peabody book store in Baltimore, floor to ceiling bookcases of dusty, dog-eared volumes, where the last corner of shelves was a hinged affair, opening with a special tap into the smoky recesses of a noisy bar, a dangerous but exciting rendezvous for enlisted men.

Let me introduce you to Specialist Bradford, he's a quick study with the typewriter during the day, never splits an infinitive or dangles a participle in his reports and, by the way, he turns into a keen shot by night, brings them down with one pull of the trigger. He learned his craft in the clear air of West Texas. No better place to pick up the art of the clean kill. The enemy cannot escape once Bradford zeros in. We would be lost without Bradford, our best man.

# A Pathway Out of Paris

The farther off from England
the nearer is to France,
so turn not pale, beloved snail,
but come and join the dance.
— *Lewis Carroll*

EVEN THOUGH WE WERE ON THE edge of spring, it snowed the night before, six inches of desiccated white covering the whole parade ground. Late snows in Germany came down from the Arctic, picking up little moisture, delivering a foot-freezing cold that melted into nothing. As I walked from the men's quarters towards the office, I looked up at Major Colton's office. He was the commander of the detachment where we lived, as opposed to Colonel Rosscommon, who was in charge of where we worked and the work we did.

Colton had seen me walking and signaled for me to wait, to talk to him. With effort, he opened the casement window that had been closed since last summer and called, "Bradford. Come up here before going to headquarters. I'll write a pass if you're late."

I came around and was let into his office by Sergeant-Major Tetley. I stood at attention in front of his desk, as was customary.

"At ease, Bradford. I hear you're an artist."

"I hope to be a painter, sir. You must have seen the easel in my room."

"Sergeant-major told me. A first for these quarters. That Corporal Selmire brought in a harpsichord a few months ago and there are several Martin guitars, but no easel before you."

"I guess it's all right, sir?"

"It's fine, Bradford. Take a seat."

He sorted through some papers on his desk and pulled one out. He read the letter to himself slowly, clearly unhappy with its contents. What did this have to do with me?

He said, "As if we did not have enough to do, high command has decided to sponsor a poster contest."

"Poster contest?"

"Some chaplains have overheard you soldiers using coarse language, so they want to encourage your clean speech with posters. It's officially entitled *USAREUR Command First Annual Clean Speech Poster Contest*. Two weeks ago Sergeant-Major posted this on the bulletin board, but not a single fucking one of you soldiers has submitted a poster."

"So you want me to draw a poster?"

"Smart man. How about three posters? I want high command to notice our entries, to leave us alone. There are prizes if you win, and, shit, I'll give you a three-day pass just for entering."

"That's very generous, sir."

"Go to it, Bradford. Posters on my desk by the end of the week."

That afternoon after work I went to the Supply Room for poster materials. Cardboard, black ink, brushes and pens. Images were swirling around in my head.

"These don't sound like supplies for the Historical Section

to me," the famously grumpy Supply Sergeant said, looking at my request list. All the goods on his shelves were his own personal, valuable property, not to be spread about willy-nilly. Every request required an official reason.

"A poster, sergeant. Three posters, actually. Major's wishes. No, major's orders."

He found everything I needed. I carried the pile back to my quarters on the third floor and had trepidations about my ideas. Since Bad Issel was known as the Army's spy outfit, espionage seemed to be the proper theme for all three. I first drew in the cartoon spy figures and then the lettering across the top of each of the placards. If the Puritan-simple message in each of them was commonplace and unimaginative, I was sure that they would please Colton.

There was time left to join the regulars at the club. It was snowing again as I walked across the parade ground, stamped my feet by the door and took a stool next to Callard at the bar.

He asked, "Bradford, where have you been? We're all ahead of you."

"You won't believe it. Three clean-speech posters."

"I saw that contest on the bulletin board. You're such a suck-up."

"Colton gave me an ultimatum. No posters, no happiness. He promised a three-day pass just for entering, though."

"I should enter too."

"The pass was for the dutiful son, Callard. Not the profligate."

"The dutiful brown-nose, you mean. You're so very clean and virginal, you'll probably win." He pinched my check and made a kiss-kiss face.

After more beers, I made my way back to our wing of Schloss Issel. Sleep always came quickly for me after a few hours at the club. Callard's night had just begun, however, and he headed down the hill to the streetcar and the Polish Quarter, where the whole troupe from the Stuttgart Ballet would be arriving.

The next morning, Colton accepted my submissions as he looked at them in turn with a different pained expression for each. Good to his word, he wrote out a three-day pass, dates at my discretion. I thought about possible vacations: it was too short a time for Rome or London, but maybe, appended to a week-end, just right for five days in Paris.

I forgot the poster contest and the three-day pass as the weeks went by. There was a spring wind when Colton waved to me again. He came to the open window and said, "First, Second and Honorable Mention, Bradford. You won them all. High command must have seen something that I didn't."

"I'm as surprised as you, sir."

"Actually, I don't think anybody else entered. Come by after five for your prizes."

He had a stack of envelopes each with a three-day pass from Detachment, Battalion and Headquarters. Another envelope bulged with four hundred dollars in Army scrip. It was the jackpot.

"Nine three-day passes, Bradford, and I guess I'll have to make good on the one I gave you. Shit, that's a month away from duty."

"Can I give them to somebody else?"

"Yes, but I wouldn't sell them if I were you."

"No, I was thinking of taking Callard and Follum to Paris for a week. There's enough money and time off for all of us."

"How does somebody get on your good side, Bradford?"

"It's better than traveling alone, sir."

"You'll lose your virginity in big, bad Paris. At least you and Follum will; Callard's went by the roadside years ago."

At the Historical Section, Captain McQuire grumbled about having so many analysts away at the same time. Three of us gone together made a big hole in our mission. Why did we expect these favors, one after the other? It tested her big heart, she said.

Callard asked, "What if we bring you back some *Chanel Number Five*, Captain?"

"Blatant bribery has no place in this, Callard."

"Only a token, a very small bottle, ma'am."

"Make it a *Guerlain* fragrance, then. *Mon Caprice* suits the taller woman."

To arrive in Paris by Saturday morning, we left right after duty on Friday in the Mercedes sedan. Callard had filled the bud-vases with new roses, again clipped from the cemetery. I had exchanged the four hundred dollars of Army scrip for French Francs, two thousand of them in a pile with a rubber band. It was a ten-hour trip through the Black Forest, the Alsace, Champagne and finally the Île-de-France and Paris.

As we drove through the outskirts in the early light, I said, "I think we should stay in a really good hotel. What's a good one, Callard?"

"We can't afford to have a fine address and to drink wine, too."

"It would be so nice to fill a tub with hot-water in a white-tiled bathroom."

"Waste of money. Even the good hotels might not have much hot water."

"So where do we stay on the cheap?"

He said, "I know an Algerian hotel, *L'Auberge Mahmoud*, just two blocks off Boulevard St. Germain. Twenty francs a night for all of us."

"Bugs in the beds?"

"No, no, Muslims are very clean. I met Mahmoud in a bar last year; his family in Algiers bought the hotel for him. With it he pays tuition at the university. Beautiful eyes, Mahmoud."

We parked the car on the street and checked into the *Auberge*, which smelled of spiced rose-water and frying oil. A woman with a black scarf opened the register for us to sign, inspecting our ID papers solemnly. The only room for twenty francs was on the fourth floor, one large bed with an embroidered tree-of-life spread, a single rush-seated chair and four hooks on the back of the door. There was a corner sink in the room with the main bathroom a floor below. An overhead light was on a timer, clicking itself off after two minutes. There would be no languorous reading, pillows propped, of Verlaine verses or *The Memoirs of Saint Simon* in this room.

Callard said that he never slept in his own bed in Paris, so it was all ours. He borrowed four hundred francs from my pile and would disappear for a few days, to smoke a pipe or two, he said. It was clear why Callard did not want us to use up the communal hoard on costly hotels.

Follum and I walked the streets of the Left Bank, stopping for wine and light meals in the cafes. A lunch of *omelette fines herbs avec salade* was ten francs, a glass of wine five. Follum was patient with me when I asked to explore the many art galleries, studying what I hoped for myself in the years to come. He was more interested in the rows of espaliered pears and apples in the Luxembourg Gardens, reminders of the farm. We discovered a small club below street level where the patrons snapped their fingers instead of applauding for the guitarist, an insomniac landlady in the floors above rumored to have forbidden the clapping of hands.

Small bistros with affordable menus on blackboards welcomed Americans, the Liberation of Paris not forgotten in twelve years. I sent a postcard to Luanna and Henry Zilbert, to tease them with my new urbanity. If they thought that they were so very happy on Water Street, then they should know that I was having glass after glass of *vin rouge* on the Left Bank, much happier with my chums. The days melted into the nights, one museum into another, the boulevards into the small streets.

It threatened to rain on our last afternoon in Paris, so we retreated to the fourth floor room, pulling the curtain across the single window. The water coursed down the glass and made a muffled tapping sound on the mansard roof.

Follum took off all his damp clothes and lay on the embroidered spread, face up, saying he had only one more change of clothes and must not get them rumpled. His hairy chest was like a layer of clothes, a blond mat, thinning to bare skin around his waist, then picking up again on his legs.

"I wonder what Callard is doing," I asked as I hung my clothes on another hook.

"Bad things."

"Probably. Let's just nap a while and maybe the rain will stop."

"I like the sound."

I lay down beside Follum and wondered where Callard would fit if he did decide to bed with us. Warmth radiated from Follum's body, I could feel it without touching him. His eyes were closed, but I could see he was aroused by my presence as he grew erect without trousers for restraint.

Turning on my side, I faced Follum and watched him. He kept his eyes shut as he became more and more prepared for what was to follow, a beckoning sign, a living omen, I thought. I put my hand over on him and his skin was smooth, firm. His eyes flickered under the lids. Not moving my hand at all, I enclosed him lightly in my curled fingers.

After many seconds that way, he turned his head and opened his eyes. "Is this a good idea?" he asked.

"It feels so good it must be."

"I have wanted you for a long time."

"Me, too, Eric."

If joy had been waiting in the darkness to start his dance, the performance that afternoon began with leaps and turns in a choreography of desire. Now that it had started, the dance continued through all of the convoluted steps until its end. I did not know what I expected from an afternoon in bed with Follum but it made my mind drive into places I could not have summoned before. What did bonding mean, becoming one with another? Was this what fusion meant, two selves blending into a single new one? How could a few hours foreshadow a life together? Did one act of love imply a thousand more? Nothing seemed impossible then, nothing hopeless. I felt fiercely protective, and completely protected at the same time.

When we had spent all energy, I went to the sink in the corner and dampened a small towel, washed the body that had given me such delight. Follum watched me with no expression on his face as I slid the towel over him. I wiped dry the hair below his knee and kissed him there.

"It *was* a mistake," he said.

"Things won't be the same."

"That's what I mean. How can we go back to Bad Issel and be just soldiers again?"

"I'm not sure we ever were 'just' soldiers."

"We should walk out of Paris tonight and down to the coast. Leave the car on the street for Callard. People went on foot all over Europe after the war, fleeing the unknown, looking for happiness, sometimes finding it. We'll take a boat across to Tangier. Callard wouldn't mind; he might even follow us there. You've got a little money, and we could find work once we're there. I'm good at a lot of things."

"There's one thing I know you're very good at."

He ignored me and continued, "I can be a waiter or a carpenter or a stone mason. You can paint, become world famous. We'll find a house on the edge of town with a small garden where I can grow vegetables. Carrots, potatoes, lettuces with red edges and herbs to make ointments. We'll live together until we look like old Moroccans, a new century begun. When people ask for the renowned artist, the locals will say walk to the end of the lane until you see two very happy men. One of them is the painter Bradford."

"Let's go have a drink, think about it."

"The Army can't make us come back from Tangier, can they?"

"I don't think so, Eric. But slow down, let's talk about it."

"I know you feel the same way. This is it and it will never happen again."

"I do feel that way," I said.

"So, let's leave now, walk south to the sea before we talk ourselves out of it."

"Deserters? Gay deserters? Being hunted for the rest of our lives?"

How was it that a farm boy was more passionate, more willing to risk it all than one raised on novels secretly taken from the high shelves and on the over-heard secrets between the grown-ups? Did the Wisconsin countryside have the perfect soil for obsessive love?

He said, "If we wait, Callard will come back and tell us we are crazy. It was just a piece of ass, he'll say, an afternoon in the sack. We'll go back to Bad Issel and the same life as before."

"It won't be exactly the same."

"No, now I'll know that everyone can see my heart beating," he said.

"Get dressed, Eric. We need a glass of wine."

The rain had stopped and our talk at the café table turned to practical matters and the feared outcomes of such a trip. What would we do for money when it ran out in Tangier, could infidels find jobs in the land of Islam, was Greece the better place to go, did the Greeks have laws that returned military deserters for prosecution, how could we make our families worry so and what about Melanie?

We did not walk down to the coast and disappear into North Africa. What had bloomed for an afternoon wilted a bit with the second carafe of wine. We looked out on the streets still wet from our rainy afternoon get slowly drier, the reflections turned to the same flat gray as before the rain.

Callard reappeared the next morning, looking fit and curiously unrumpled for someone who had taken so many pipes on a three-tiered bed only a few blocks away. He had spent all the francs for his adventures, but he had not forgotten beforehand to buy a pebble-sized bottle of *Mon Caprice*. As he drove on the highway back to Bad Issel, Follum said to him, "You look better than when we arrived. How can you dip into danger without paying the price? It isn't fair."

"Who said I don't pay underneath, in my hidden heart and who said life was fair?" He looked straight forward, hands on the wheel.

"It doesn't seem to be."

Callard asked, "Didn't you get laid, Follum? That's what Paris is all about."

Follum looked over his shoulder at me in the back seat while Callard chattered on about those who must pay and those who do not. Life had its darlings, he said, and it was not his fault if he was one. I knew that if life was not treating Follum and me fairly, at least it had given us a chance. That beautiful pathway out of Paris, lined with tall greenery and hope, closed in on itself as it had opened, like a mirage fading when the temperature cooled. It was there for a moment, though, a glimmering vista to another land, a world of sensual joy, replete with the aroma of citrus, absinthe and Follum's love forever. A trail we could have taken. Would it offer itself again?

At the German frontier, while Callard dealt with the customs, I emptied the bud-vases into the trash barrel, the red roses dried to a hard brown. The next morning as I walked past Major Colton's office on the way to duty, he came to the window and called down, his voice full of amusement.

"I suppose you lost every bit of your prize money, Bradford?"

"All of it, sir."

"Your lily-white virginity. Did you lose that and find true love?"

"I think so, I'm not sure."

"Shit, I suppose she had hair on her legs."

"Lots of it, sir."

# Cooking on a Gas Ring

> Happiness makes up in height
> for what it lacks in length.
> — *Robert Frost*

WITH DOSSIER IN HAND, THE Countess von Kravitz paused at my desk. "Paris was good for you and Follum, I can see," she said.

"A pathway opened, Katherine."

"I've noticed a lingering, a touching that wasn't there before."

"There's no fooling the Viennese, is there?"

"Especially in matters of heart's desire."

"Follum and I are guilty, I confess."

She pulled the dossier against her chest and sat lightly on the edge of the desk, exuding a confidential air. "I have wanted to cook a dinner for the two of you, and now the opportunity arises. A celebration evening with sauerbraten and the famous von Kravitz *Bratkartofflen.*"

"I'm sure Eric would love it and I know that I would."

"How about this Saturday evening? You haven't been to my flat before. It's an easy walk from the schloss."

"I'll bring some red wine?"

"Red is fine. We'll have time to discuss all the details of Paris." She dipped her head and gazed at me with raised eyebrows. Follum had said that everybody would see his heart beating, and here it was me with the coronary transparency.

Callard had told me Katherine's story, that she was a countess by marriage and American by birth. She met a man of thirty on the day of her graduation from a Vienna girl's school and love came upon them like a great wave, swelling over every scheme of her diplomat parents to thwart it. Only after a honeymoon in Italy did she discover her new title. The Countess von Kravitz und Kollenberg.

On Saturday evening as we left the front gates of Schloss Issel, I told Follum, "I think she somehow knows what happened in Paris."

"Did you tell her?"

"No, she has sensed it from our body language."

"Good for her. I wanted to tell her anyway," Follum said.

"If anyone can keep a secret, it's Katherine."

We walked down the hill from the schloss, the grapevines now in full leaf, the rose bushes in the cemetery cascading over the iron fence in a musky perfume. The road, which zigzagged down from the schloss, led right into the middle of the village.

The curving part beside the cemetery dipped down between two retaining walls and it felt private enough for me to put my arm around Follum as we walked. I wondered if we had gone to Morocco, could I walk hand-in-hand with Follum even in the crowded market? Was there a place like that on earth, where we could be open about our love and face no hate, no harsh laws? I thought not.

Follum was thinking the same thing. He said, "It doesn't have to be Tangier, you know. I still have family living in a village in Norway, my grandfather made me memorize its name and where it was. They would welcome us, hide us."

"I'd like Tangier better. Warm. By the sea."

"Me, too. I think about it all the time."

"Why can't we make it happen?"

He said, "Because you're afraid, worried what people will think. I know that nothing bad will happen; instead we would have a great life. The Army will forget about us, wash their hands of the trouble. I can imagine the vegetable garden in my mind, one green row next to another. Your studio is nearby, with an open window on my garden. I see you at the easel, the first colors on your painting, the aroma of turpentine. We talk back and forth."

"Paradise enow, together in the wilderness."

"You make fun, but it can happen. I know it."

We walked out of the retaining walls on the next switchback and I took my arm off his shoulders as houses with watching windows lined the road. Katherine lived just beyond the Bad Issel square with the fountain, where Callard had worked so diligently for the Mercedes money. There was an old woman with a cane near the fountain, the Mother Superior of the Black Market, I was sure, but we walked past her without pausing, no contact of eyes and into the narrow street to Katherine's flat.

I rang the bell and she buzzed the door open from above. Her part of Bad Issel had survived the intense bombing of the British, old three story, half-timbered houses now converted to apartments and shops. We walked up stairs, where she waited at the open door.

The aroma of the sauerbraten filled the apartment, three rooms with dark beams, adzed and carved. The round table was set with a white cloth and three place settings, old silver and porcelain plates. She was wearing a long dress with a high collar, a deep maroon red, with a necklace of garnets. Away from the metal desks of the Historical Section, Katherine was a glamorous woman, elegant and poised. She could have been born an Austrian, her blonde hair still abundant, her pale blue eyes accented with a dark circle around each pupil.

She said, "You're late. I wondered if you had decided to forget our dinner and instead took the night train to the South of France, never to be seen again. New clothes, new names, new lives."

Follum said, "We were talking about something very like that."

"As I thought about it, I worried at first that you had, then worried that you hadn't."

I said, "We talk ourselves out of it, or more correctly, I talk us out of it."

"Probably the wise path. Time is on your side; the Cote d'Azur will still be there next year."

Follum said, "We keep using Tangier as the destination of desire."

"Tangier. Karl and I spent several months there in the early thirties, before the war started calling up all the Austrian young men. I remember it as a paradise. We swam in the sea every day, ate wonderful meals with fresh vegetables and roasted chicken from those tall terracotta pots. The people were gentle, proud to be Tangerines, not citizens of the odious Spanish Morocco. I often wonder if we had stayed on in Morocco, pushing deeper south past the Atlas Mountains as the war approached, hiding from the world in those hill villages, protecting our happiness… what would have happened?"

Follum looked strongly at me while she talked. I was the fearful one, I knew, afraid of being caught and brought back to the stockade for punishment. The first part of a longer, more somber thought occurred as he watched me, that I did not love Eric enough. If I did, we would have already fled to the south several weeks ago from Paris. I was unable to summon enough love, a weakling, like being without the stamina to walk the tall hill, so never to see the fine view. Would I ever have the strength to give love without hesitation?

I said, "It's me who puts on the brakes, Katherine. Eric would be planting his beets and carrots and I would be facing a new canvas now, if it weren't for my fears."

"There's a cork-screw for your wine in the kitchen, Harold. Let's have a toast to Tangier, the once and future place."

Katherine presented her sauerbraten dinner with ease, bringing small platters from the kitchen. We spooned the portions for ourselves: the sliced meat, the Von Kravitz roast potatoes, quartered Sicilian pickles, cabbage cooked in wine vinegar. The dinner plates were porcelain with the gold rims almost rubbed away, the ornate initials K.u.K. turned to face each chair.

Our first bottle of red ran dry and she produced another for the rest of the meal. We helped her clear the plates to what she called the kitchen, an adjoining room with a double gas ring for cooking, open shelves for plates and bowls, a sink with cold water, a narrow center table and a window ledge for keeping butter and milk cool outside.

She said, "Both of you sit down and I'll bring in the strudel, from the bakery two houses down. And there's some Turkish coffee that my felonious mother-in-law is never without."

When we had finished the dessert, I asked, "Katherine, you must have had a good marriage. I'm sorry that the war took your husband."

"We had six good years, more than many Europeans at that time. Karl was very handsome, very kind and I was mad for him. My parents in the States refused to let us come back, invalidated our visas as the war gained momentum and we gave our steamship tickets from Lisbon to a neighbor family. After that, nobody got out."

Follum said, "I'm surprised that an American citizen could not get out."

"I could have, I'm sure. When Karl was given his

commission, I *chose* to stay, to look after his mother and aunts. In fact, they looked after me when Karl was killed in nineteen forty-four. After the Allies came, there was a great need for a person with fluent German, especially one with an American birth certificate."

"Would you go back to the States now? I'm sure it's possible."

"No, I haven't forgiven my parents yet. I don't know if I ever can. It's very fortunate that I have the job at Schloss Issel. I think I can work there for a few years more, and then I may go to the South of France or Tangier, too. I should think that you both will be established there by then, planting and painting. I can take a back room by the month in your house, write my novel."

I said, "Callard says that the Section could not run without the captain or the countess."

"The title is amusing to me now, worth so very little. There are dozens of us countesses now cooking sauerbraten on gas rings and cooling milk outside the window."

I said, "If you ever need money, Katherine, we always have a little to spare."

"Thank you, my dears, but the civilian pay at Schoss Issel is adequate, not generous, but enough that I can eat in restaurants on occasion, buy a new scarf and take the train to Vienna to visit Karl's family every other month. From time to time, the captain sees fit to include me on some of her adventures, for notably good extra pay."

"Callard also says you should get a raise. That you're one of the few who really knows the scope of the project, keeps it going."

"Let's not talk about it; I signed a pledge not to."

"Of course."

She continued, "The irony is that the Schloss Issel was owned until the nineteenth century by close relatives of the von Kravitz family. They sold the Schloss Issel to the Dowager

Duchess of Wurttemberg, Hitler took over in the nineteen thirties and the allies moved in after the armistice. My mother-in-law says that I might have been both the Countess Kravitz und Kollenberg *and* the Countess Issel if certain people died before others. The Austrians, strict about rank and title, would have to address me, Countess Countess.

I said, "I will do that from now on."

"You mustn't. It amuses me as I sit in my desk in the Historical Section. We have a friend in Vienna, a dear old man, who had three separate degrees in medicine. We must address him as Doktor Doktor Doktor. He never asks us not to, but if he is in a good mood, he replies Danke Danke Danke."

It was late when we left Katherine's flat, both Follum and I savoring Katherine's company. At the schloss, we looked for moment at each other, and then went to our separate rooms.

Parsons was still awake, the two others asleep. He had papers spread out over his bed and was writing on a card held high on a stack of books.

He said, whispering to not wake our roommates, "Bradford, I'm getting married in a couple of weeks. To Inga. Will you be the best man?"

Inga was his sleep-over girl friend. It was said that you could not master the fine points of the German language without sleeping next to it, playing with its boobies during the night. Parson was close to fluency, everybody said.

I said, "Yes, of course. Are those the invitations?"

"To the reception over at the Bierstube Langenscheidt. I borrowed your address book, I apologize. Everybody's street address is in it, not like mine."

"It's okay. So you'll be moving out, getting an apartment on the economy?"

"Doesn't that sound great?"

"Marriage is not on my list of great, must-do activities, Parsons. I will miss you here and our summer trip to Switzerland."

He thought for a moment, then said, "Maybe we can do that trip anyway. Inga has to work, you know."

# <u>Sand in an Oyster</u>

It is a double pleasure to
deceive the deceiver.
— *Jean de La Fontaine*

THE CAPTAIN SAID, "I'VE BEEN talking with Katherine, and she has a plan, a classic, elegant bit of counterintelligence. She and I, with you and Follum will drive to Austria day after tomorrow. We will check into the historic Eisenstiefel Inn in Ittelsdorf, ostensibly we'll be the American remainder of an old Austrian family, the ill-assorted stump, searching out our roots in the Old Country."

I said, "The Austrians are too clever to be fooled by one of our gray-painted Army sedans."

"That's why we've included you and Follum. The Mercedes four-door you own with Callard is still registered to the Stalingrad hero. We've checked that. If the Austrians research the plates, which we are sure they will, they will find patriotic, old-line German family owners."

"And when we're there?"

"We will find the Nazi oscillating triggers. The last scientists alive in nineteen forty-five buried them in a field somewhere between Plentersheim and Ittelsdorf."

I asked, "So we just start digging?"

"Katherine came up with this. Instead of asking about the possibility of buried devices, she will pass it around that *she* has an actual device for sale. An oscillating trigger from the estate of her husband's uncle, the nuclear scientist Von Kravitz who disappeared in the days after the surrender. What good does it do her in the basement safe? She needs money now, cannot wait forever. Who wants to buy it?"

"Do we know what it looks like?"

"No, and Katherine will be vague about its provenance. By putting a price on it, and placing it on the open market, those with their buried triggers can expect their profits to be cut to nothing if she is first to sell. Only one version is needed by the west. Once it is sold, the others are worthless. We are hoping to create a race in Ittelsdorf to sell it before Katherine, to bring the culprits out in the open."

Western scientists had invented their own fuses for bludgeoning a nuclear device into exploding, but the elegant oscillating trigger, concocted by Germans in the last years of the war, fooled the bomb with ordinary household current, rising and falling in a brilliantly simple pattern, then ka-boom. Trouble-free as a toaster. We have been directed to find it; the safety of the entire West is at stake.

The captain relished the idea of such a mission. She would create an innocent-appearing Austrian family and bring the members into the thick of things. Follum and I searched that night in the supply room and the Covert Supplies stores for clothing that did not say American Spy. There were Russian and German uniforms from all years, all ranks, coveralls with the names of plumbing repair companies, civilian attire of all manner.

Callard helped us with his eye for German dress and he found outfits for Follum and me like an opera costumer, placing items on clothes hangers against us in turn. He chose pieces in Bavarian grey wool with touches of forest green, long trousers and a change with short pantaloons, thick gray socks, and awkward post-war German shoes. Other outfits had a quasi-military look, dark green shirts with fine black piping, and the trousers that matched.

There were loden coats, one in a poisonous avocado, with stag-horn closures and the other one in all black. All Austrians wore hats, so he picked several varieties, a severe high-peaked felt hat for me, with a cluster of black feathers.

As I laced up the German brogans, I said, "Callard, I feel like Mario Lanza in the *Student Prince*, singing Heidelberg drinking songs. Nobody believed that he was German, either."

He said, "Follum and you both have the right Teutonic look, blond gullibility. It can't be faked. The clothes may be too clean, but we'll muss them up. Spill some *Forty-seven Eleven* on them. Put salt stains on your shoes. I'll fabricate some dribbles from oxtail soup, brownish spots with bits of onion. Anyway, you're supposed to be American boys of good, loyal stock, back to absorb the wonders of the Fatherland. These are family clothes you brought along to ingratiate your relatives."

Follum looked every inch the Austrian, the product of long lines of heartless generals. He was frightening in his genuineness, the avocado loden a perfect fit. I was sure that everyone would see through my facade, but Callard said I could pass, if I kept my mouth shut.

It took a long day of driving to get to the Eisenstiefel Inn in Ittelsdorf. We were the loving family on an Austrian outing, only by chance there with a purpose. Katherine would search out the perfect place to introduce her bit of information, like inserting the irritating grain of sand into a pearl oyster. It would fester for a while, be coated with nacre, then open to reveal what we wanted.

The inn was dark-paneled and smoky, the windows looking

out over the famous trout-stream to the foothills beyond. Even on the verge of summer, fireplaces were needed to keep the chill out of the low-ceilinged rooms. Captain McQuire chatted with the desk people, splaying across the counter our fake passports with the last name Gausmann, and the rumpled steamship tickets. Katherine presented her own papers, a family member caught in Europe during the fighting. The desk people filed the visas and tickets away in an office drawer. Certain villagers would surely enquire about the details of our arrival and the validity of our papers.

The hotel director surveyed the unlikely quartet we were and switched to English. "We welcome the family Gausmann. Yours is an Austrian family name?"

McQuire said, "Our mother was a von Kollenberg, imminently Austrian, but that was many generations back. Katherine is searching for several branches of the family tree."

"I believe there are still von Kollenbergs in this area. I will ask."

"How kind. The boys and I will be hiking every day, a longstanding family sport, but Katherine may have time to meet with them. She remembers a great-great aunt from Vienna, born here, we think."

We went to bed early, all of us fatigued from the long drive. I looked over at Follum with the first arousals of lust, but the late hour and sleep won.

McQuire, Follum and I took a mountain hike the next day, starting after breakfast until well beyond noon. If village eyes followed our progress, we presented the picture of a hardy, outdoor-loving trio in well-burnished hiking clothes, laughing together and pointing to the high destinations where patches of snow still lingered.

In a shop near the hotel, McQuire had purchased a hazelnut walking-stick, crooked and well-polished, and she made much of her new hiking rhythm, stick out forward, then backward.

Follum just looked at me and I raised my eyebrows, but we hurried to keep up with the windmill of activity ahead of us, in her trailing scent of *Mon Caprice*, up across the foothills to the high meadows beyond.

Clouds gathered late in the morning, so we barely made it back down to the Eisenstiefel before the heavy rain. Katherine met us for lunch, our table with a view out the casements, across the stream with the famous trout lurking just below the surface.

McQuire asked, "Anything, Katherine?"

"The bierstube is the town gathering place, all the old women at the bakery and the market agree. We should go late this afternoon. Let's take naps and meet back here at sixteen thirty."

I tried not to gulp down the coffee at the end of the meal. The thought of an afternoon nap with Follum, before the family gathering, brought sensual waves through my body. We walked with exaggerated restraint up the stairs to the first landing, then after turning the corner, both of us sprinting up the next stairs. We locked the door to our room and pulled off our scratchy woolens, too thick to rumple in a pile on the floor.

Follum's body was firm and warm as I explored it again, kissing it and covering it with gentle bites. Follum's fake complaints of hurt only urged me on. Why were we not in Tangier doing this, like Follum wanted, the sound of the sea waves coming through the open window and the aroma of spiced lemons from the marketplace below? Desire fought again with sensibility; for two hours, desire won.

At the bierstube, we joined the large table with other families. Katherine did the talking, in her High German clipped tones. The final consonant of one word was razor-cut from the beginning vowel of the next like an Alpine peak, distinct and dangerous in the thin air. The women watched Katherine with a sharp awareness, she obviously a prime example of the highest Teutonic caste. If they did not like her, they gave into her perfect, upper-echelon diction. She introduced each of us in turn, with shaking of hands across the table.

It was hard for me to understand her precision German, but if I relaxed the tensed muscles behind my ears, I could start to hear single words and phrases. She talked about Follum and me, her nephews, dear fellows with not so much as a syllable of decent German, which brought laughter and nods our way. I could pick out a discourse about no money, hard times after the war, and the plight of patriotic women. McQuire, her good cousin, just nodded and smiled, interjecting a few words now and then. Katherine was the skipper of this ship.

She asked questions of all the women there, ignoring the few old men. It would be hard to say that the village women warmed to Katherine, but they did not miss a word of what she said. They gave into her forceful running of the afternoon like a town meeting.

I finally heard the words for uncle and gift and invention. Then, she went on with more about the Gausmanns, the wonderful old grandmother with a lace collar from Cologne, the train out of Germany to Portugal in the early 30s. She ended this tour-de-force with a question if anybody knew where she could sell this valuable gift, a scientific inheritance really, to get the Gausmann family back on track?

She looked at us with a we're-ready-to-go look. We all stood up with smiles and bows, shaking hands again and left the bierstube. The only true warmth in the bierstube came from the fireplace.

As we walked back to the Inn, Katherine said, "It's done. I think I made a connection and we'll have a response soon."

The captain asked, "Was it that old woman with the short white hair? Black eyes? She immediately understood what you were talking about."

"Yes. Her husband was a professor, she said. Tubingen, then Berlin."

The captain said, "Katherine, you made it sound so every-day, nothing to it. I have a bomb part in my purse, does anybody want it? A hundred thousand marks, for the family Gausman, you know. Good people. A Vicki Baum novel."

Katherine told us that she learned much from the dowager countess, sitting in on her entertainments in Vienna, her guests powerless to keep secret the information that she wanted. She could pry an embedded bit out without the victim feeling any hint of the sharpness of her instrument, her ever-handy tray of scalpels and forceps disguised as cake forks and coffee spoons. After an hour of her short-cake rounds with Alpen-berry frosting and hot Istanbul coffee, no secret, not even the one hidden the farthest from the light, escaped the dowager's grasp.

Katherine left a telephone number in Vienna at the inn, should anybody from the village need it for "information." It was the dowager countess' number, with an immediate connection to our people. The captain decided that is was better to play the soft pedal with this, let the bogus information percolate through the village.

In the previous years, our agents thought that the triggers might be buried behind monastery walls, but blue-eyed monks were shocked at the suggestion of their holy stonework brought into question. Then, testimony at a Nuremberg trial revealed the triggers might be hidden in the fields near Ittelsdorf or Plentersheim, family homes to several scientists. Nothing, however, could be found.

We drove back to Schloss Issel the next day and waited. Several weeks went by with our regular work at the Historical Section taking on a new charge every time the phone rang in the captain's office. I don't believe the other workers knew what was transpiring, the news the four of us were awaiting. After a month with no reply, the phone rings did not jolt us awake with expectation.

And it was not the telephone that brought the news.

Katherine found a short article in the back pages of *Der Spiegel*. The headline in German said *Allied Intelligence Steals German Device*. She translated it aloud: "Informants for this magazine have discovered that the mysterious oscillating trigger, long known as a valuable German invention in the years before the war, was coveted by the Allied scientists, unable to replicate a simple German professor's work. The trigger was purchased by an unidentified agent of US Intelligence from Frau Helga Koenig, the widow of the illustrious nuclear scientist, Heinz Koenig. Frau Koenig could not reveal the selling price, but said it was very low, almost a theft of German patrimony, like stealing an original Beethoven score. Professor Koenig was killed in a building collapse by a low-level British bomb 1945, along with the entire medical staff and patients of the Berlin Children's Hospital, under which the nuclear laboratories had long been sited for reasons of national economy. The widow Koenig lives simply in Ittelsdorf with her mother."

So the grain of sand, inserted with care at the right place in the mollusk, rubbing and irritating the tender flesh, produced a shiny pearl.

# ON THE FLOOR IN BERLIN

Delusion, error, fallacy, hallucination, illusion, phantasm.
All the words listed above agree in denoting something which
appears to be true,
but which is really false.
— *Funk & Wagnall's Handbook of Synonyms.*

WE WERE TAKEN TO OUR ROOM
in the safe-house by the housekeeper and she stood erect by the
door, oozing a mixture of power and subservience that Mrs.
Flack could not have begun to imagine.

Callard said, "Frau Munster, good to see you again."

"Herr Callard."

"Are the sheets all folded tight and starched like the last
trip?"

"They are perfect, Herr Ballad. Fräulein Untermeyer has
worked late to get them just right."

"Is the window ajar like I instructed? For the fresh air?"

"Two centimeters. For the fresh air."

"And the bath-tub is without a ring?"

"Like a Swiss surgery, Herr Callard."

"The toilet lid up?"

"Up, as you request."

I detected a smirk on her face as she stood with military uprightness and I knew I heard a taunting tone in Callard's voice. It was a waltz the two had danced before, I was sure, and a difficult call as to who was leading and who following.

He continued, "White gloves running along every edge?"

"Every edge."

"Good work, then, Frau. You may go." She turned smartly on his dismissive tone and walked briskly down the hall. Did I hear the metallic click of heels?

I said, "Callard, you shouldn't tease her."

"Germans understand being teased, their authority brought into question. They can feel out their position in the scheme of things, the danger of your hot breath."

"She did seem to get excited, almost like a sexual act."

"If I only had the right uniform, more like the olden times with a sweat-stained riding crop and golden-edged epaulets. She would be whimpering."

"Stop it, Callard."

"It's a game, Bradford. Germans distrust democracy, but they love it when an *Übermensch* with clever eyes circles them slowly and questions down into their very soul."

"I guess I have noticed that."

"Of course you have. They will hate you if you don't play your part, so narrow your eyes and polish your boots."

The housekeepers at all fifty of our safe-houses were widows whose husbands had been killed by the Russians; their loyalty to the Allies was varied, strong enough to pass investigation, but their hatred of the Soviets was endless and deep. For their own safety, we called every one of them Frau Munster, and if it was a large house with a dozen or more bedrooms, she would have a young cleaning girl, inevitably called Fräulein Untermeyer.

Callard and I were staying in Berlin House No. 23 in one

of the villa suburbs, an Italianate mansion set within a steel-fenced garden of large trees. Neighbors surely knew the cars that arrived and left through the automated gates were American military, but like the different comings and goings of the 20s, 30s and 40s, it was better not to pay too much attention. We had come to Berlin with Captain McQuire on a courier trip, taking the train across the Soviet part of Germany, leaving from the Osterbahnhof several miles east of Frankfurt.

High command did not trust flights over East Germany; an engineered crash could divulge too much, briefcases spread across the countryside. So documents had to go by train to Berlin, with an armed officer and usually two enlisted men. Our couriers were never stopped or questioned, the Soviets aware that their own agents would be immediately stopped in retribution, spiraling into myriad acts of reprisal. This balance of fear assured that papers would get through. It was assumed as many Soviet agents with secret papers crossed West Germany every day as ours crossed over to Berlin.

We made no effort to disguise our identity, as we had on trips to Switzerland or Luxembourg, although we did wear civilian clothes. The captain carried the faux crocodile briefcase, never relinquishing its handle. I wondered if the Army was overworking fake crocodile. With a great deal of checking of papers by border guards, writing down the numbers of identity cards, we sat on the shuttered train for the five hour trip through to the Berlin HauptBahnhof.

We were met by a car and driven to a gated compound where the briefcase was given up, and then the driver took us to House No. 23 on Leydenstrasse. There were a dozen bedrooms in the house for an assortment of Counterintelligence enlisted personnel, a lounge with upholstered chairs, a dining room and a library with sparsely filled shelves of books, novels in German, travel guides in Polish and Hungarian.

Outside of the front door, McQuire conferred with Callard

over a small package from which he extracted something and put it into the cigarette package in his shirt. It looked like a short piece of dark string. McQuire smiled as Callard put it into his shirt pocket and then she went on to the officers' safe house, farther down the Leydenstrasse.

It was late afternoon when Frau Munster left us, so I took a nap before the evening that Callard promised. After several hours, at ten, we ordered a car to take us to the Spion Bar on the Hindenstrasse line of night clubs. The Spion was built as a small amphitheatre with booths along each level, and a long bar where the stage customarily went; since the occupants of every booth could see those in other booths as well as those at the bar it was a perfect arrangement for people-watching. We found two empty stools at the bar, looked back up at the booths, now filled with Berliners of all ages, smoking and laughing. A gypsy orchestra played Hungarian songs while the telephones rang.

Callard said, "Riddled with spies from every country, East and West."

"So why are we here?"

"To be in the middle of things."

The booths had telephones with numbered signs above, so the other booths could call someone they found attractive. Table Thirteen here, wave if you see us, which we did. Also, there was a note-pad and pencil at each booth for private notes to a desired one across the room. Waiters were tipped to take the folded papers from booth to booth. Several telephones and pads were spaced along the bar.

Callard said, "If you can't get laid here, you belong in a monastery."

"Is it safe to rendezvous with other people here?"

"Nothing's safe, Bradford." As it was so often when I was with Callard, I felt like a flour-sack farm girl on her first city outing.

The telephone near us rang and Callard answered. He

turned around and waved to two men on the top tier. They waved back. Callard sent them a note, tipping the waiter two marks. In a few minutes a startling proposition came back. Callard wagged his forefinger at them, naughty, naughty, and turned his attention away.

"Prick teasing, Bradford. That's what we're doing tonight."

So we sat for several hours, fielding calls and sending notes back and forth. Drinks arrived with more offers attached, such as a ride to the late night party on Staffelstrasse. Everybody would be there and American soldiers would be highly appreciated. I wondered why Callard did not pursue some of the offers; he was so much in his element. Two Russian officers made calls to Callard individually, to no avail, and several single women pressed their cause with written notes, one with a crisp hundred Deutschmark bill enclosed, which he sent back. He was never so shy or uncommitted in the Polish quarter of Stuttgart, with much less enthusiasm from the other end. Just after midnight, we left. A curious evening where money and sex merged together, the strong aroma of thwarted lust.

The next morning at breakfast Callard said we must go back to the Spion, he had lost the microfilm that McQuire had given him for safekeeping. It just came out of his pocket with one of the cigarettes. So foolish, he said.

At the bar, which was not officially open, we went in the alleyway door and Callard told the bartender we had lost something of value.

"What, exactly? Was it a watch?" he asked.

"No, like a piece of string. Five inches long."

"An ordinary piece of string?"

"No, a special piece. Quite valuable. We'll look along the carpet with our flashlight. It will reflect the light. A shiny sort of string, actually."

For half we hour, we crawled under and around the stools with the flashlight, the bar gloomier during the day than at night. We found nothing, even though the waiters joined us searching on the floor. Callard went to the bartender to evidence his distress and to give his name and address, should anything turn up.

In the car back, Callard said, "That was most agreeable."

"What's going on?"

"It's best you don't know. The Tibetan Prayer Wheel is so painful that you would tell them everything."

Callard explained to McQuire about the loss of the string in the train back to Frankfurt, and she seemed unconcerned as well, almost pleased about it. I was mystified, but kept my silence.

Weeks later, Callard told me what had happened that night. The lost piece of string was a length of microfilm containing disparaging reports about our U-2 flights, formal complaints prior to an investigation about the fuzziness of the photographs, letters from the unhappy pilots themselves, reprimands and a dozen or more actual examples of out-of-focus pictures over Soviet targets. They were all false, created to convince the Soviets of the ineptness of our surveillance project.

As Schloss Issel knew, quite the opposite was true. The U-2 photographs were so sharp we could read the license plate numbers on moving automobiles. The false reports were inserted all over Europe, our Spion Bar episode only one of many. The Russians postponed shooting-down attempts just long enough for our cartographers to establish the exact positions every city and military base, the whole of Russia at last mapped down to the last foot.

Callard said, "It comes so naturally to dissemble. I worry what will become of us, Bradford."

# Polska Keilbasa

Marriage is a wonderful invention;
but, then again, so is a bicycle repair kit.
— *Billy Connolly*

PARSONS WAS VISIBLY NERVOUS.
He had been married that morning to Inga by a bow-tied German official at the Rathaus, her family and his friends encircling, nobody smiling very much. After the ceremony, Parsons, Callard and I went ahead in the Mercedes to the Bierstube Langenscheidt's private upstairs room, checking out the arrangements for the reception to begin in a little over an hour. Inga would arrive with the others, her slow-gaited mother, family and friends by the streetcar up to Bad Issel, then the steep walk up the hill to the bierstube.

It was another hot afternoon of the summer. A vast high pressure system sat above the Alps, circulating slowly clockwise to bring the Saharan air through the Swiss passes to the wilted southern cities of Germany. Day followed day with no cool respite, the mere idea of a wind vacationing on other continents. Tempers flared and newspapers reported that murders soared all across the south, crazed citizens boiling over and at long last doing in their odious mothers-in-law or their rackety neighbors.

The tables in the bierstube reception room had been pulled together into a long banquet version, making an "L" around one corner, and Katherine had arranged two bouquets of summer flowers from a friend's garden. Plates of Camembert cheese, mixed with chopped onion and paprika and bread were spaced along the table, a cake at the corner. It was only mildly festive, perhaps suitable for this inauspicious affair. What was Parsons thinking to get married?

Callard said, "Bloody hot in here. Can't we open some windows?"

"Frau Langenscheidt said no, they were screwed shut during the war," Parsons replied, wiping his forehead.

"Has she heard that the war is definitely over, that screwdrivers are for sale again? Do they have some fans, then?"

"Again, no."

"What about the champagne? Is it iced down?" It was actually not champagne but the more affordable German substitute, sparkling *Sekt*, a sweet fruity version. Parsons had purchased three cases of *Sekt* from a wine shop in Bad Issel, carried them up to the Bierstube Langenscheidt. The bottles were warm to the touch.

Parsons appeared helpless, a deer in the headlights. "Frau said they had only one tray of ice, and it was required by their downstairs, regular, customers."

Callard said, "I know where the ice house is, behind the Hauptbahnhof. Bradford, we have time to drive over there and get some ice. Hot champagne is impossible."

We ran over to the Schloss parking lot and drove the Mercedes out the front gate. It was a ten minute drive to the center, so he pressed the sedan to its utmost. We passed the open-windowed streetcar struggling uphill with a full load of be-flowered guests fanning themselves, a dozen stops left before

Bad Issel. Callard expertly maneuvered the streets behind the Hauptbahnhof, lined with concrete warehouses and steel-doored offices of shipping agents.

I asked, "I hope you have some Deutsch Marks."

"I have two hundred. Enough, surely."

"How did you know about this ice house?"

"A man from the Krakow Klub works there. I caught his attention when I told him, 'Hot hands for cold work.' We bonded that very night."

"You went with him to the ice house?"

"Only once. We had no where else to go. He had his own key. Love came into fullest bloom in deepest Siberia."

We parked against the loading dock and knocked on the door at the top of the steps. The sign said *Hausmann Wasser Eis, AG*. In several minutes the door opened partially, a man in a white shirt, collar buttoned, and black armbands asked what we wanted while he kept his hand on the knob, looking both ways down the street. The ice plant was closed for the weekend, he said. He was clearly not Callard's icy conquest from the weeks before.

Callard tried his best German, which was easy for me to understand, while Black Armband's Schwabisher-Deutsch was not. He asked why we needed ice, as it was forbidden to sell it to ordinary citizens. *Ganz Verboten.*

Callard: A wedding reception, most important in this *Uberheiss.*

Armband: We all suffer. But perhaps I can let you have a little if you have *Kleine Deuschtergelt*? (I knew this meant small bills, the natural exchange for illicit deals.)

Callard: *Natürlicht.*

Armband: Fifty marks for each block.

He looked again each way on the street. Now, I was becoming nervous, wondering how severe a crime buying ice off hours could be. Bradford, you and Callard are being charged with *Verboten Wasser Eis Ankaufen,* ten years in Prussia. Wouldn't mother be pleased?

Callard: Twenty for a block.

Armband: Forty.

Callard: Twenty-five.

Armband: Okay, *Bestimmt,* but only the four pieces.

Callard pulled out a hundred mark note. Black Armband hesitated at the single note, then pocketed it and carried the four blocks to the door on a dolly, one at a time, each weighing about thirty pounds, taper-shaped liked a small obelisk. We stacked them on the English wool robe on the back seat, folding the robe over to maintain the cool. I could see the water soaking through, darkening the plaid, melting out from under as Callard raced back to Bad Issel, the hot day having its way.

The guests arrived as we lugged the blocks upstairs, arranged for ice-picks and buckets to cool the bottles. At least thirty people were already in the reception room, most drinking beer from glass steins instead of waiting for the *Sekt* to cool. I could see the captain, the major, Katherine, and Mrs. Rosscommon talking together, a separate cluster of master sergeants and Corporal Murgon, the crowd from the Historical Section in another group, and Inga's darkly-clothed family at the far end. Natural selection at its best.

Parsons and Inga stood near one end of the table, shaking hands with well-wishers. I kissed Inga on the cheek, and she smelled of a strong cologne mixed with anxiety and perspiration.

I said, "Happy day, Parsons. Where for the honeymoon?"

"Garmisch. A special rate for Army newlyweds." That sounded even less joyful than this reception, dozens of other soldiers with their blonde brides, Teutonic lust in the thin mountain air.

I said, "It will be cooler there."

As Inga kissed the next person, Parsons said quietly, "Wasn't it nice of Horst and Wolfgang to come all the way from

Lucerne? Have you talked to them yet?"

"Good grief, Parsons. Why did you invite them?"

"I saw their names in your address book. Thought it would be good to see them again. You don't mind, do you? They especially want to talk to you."

I looked around the room, and indeed the brothers were on the far side, in the midst of Inga's family. They were both wearing black suits of thick wool on this summer day, black hats on the back of their heads. In their country way, they were both as sensual as I remembered. I could almost smell their animal musk, Wolfang's sharper than Horst's, from across the room.

I had never told Follum about my dalliance in Lucerne, hoping no reason would arise. Now that issues of loyalty and fidelity were involved, I wanted to do nothing that would injure Follum, stories of past adventures included. I would talk to the brothers, iron this out, before Follum arrived.

Horst saw me coming their way and stepped out of his group. He shook my hand with gusto and patted my shoulder at the same time. "West Texas Bradford. We are happy to see you again, looking so tan and healthy."

"Me, too, Horst. Did you take the early train from Switzerland?"

"*Ja*. It was dark when we started. Wolfgang says it will be worth it to see our Texas man again, be with you. We are staying right here at the bierstube to be close."

"Horst, I cannot. I have a friend now."

"We have many friends, too. I don't understand."

"A special friend."

"A lover, you mean? How is that possible in the American army?"

"We're secret lovers. Nobody else knows."

"Ah. But, we do now."

"Yes. Please don't give us away. We would be in trouble if you did."

"A secret you ask us to keep?" The sparkle in his eyes said maybe otherwise.

Wolfgang freed himself from Inga's family and came across to shake my hand and grasp my shoulder in the same way as Horst. Only this hand-clasp emitted a raw sexual electricity, the Black Fire that I tasted in their steamy apartment in Lucerne. The hot, physical brother instead of the talkative one. A wave of guilt came ashore in my mind, reprimanding me for hopeless promiscuity, for being a bad lover to Follum. Would he always be at risk from my changing desires?

Horst said something in German to his brother and Wolfgang whispered something back into Horst's ear.

Horst said, "Wolfgang says that you should ask your special friend to join us. We can have another night together, the four of us this time. Our room here is big. We will push the beds together."

"It won't work, Horst. Follum doesn't know about you and our night in Lucerne. He is a good man, an innocent... and here he is...now."

I could feel Follum's arm across my back. He put out his hand to Horst, "Hello, I'm Eric Follum. A friend of Harold's."

Horst said, "We understand you are friends. Special friends."

Follum looked at me in a quandary. "That's right. Special friends."

I said, "Eric, you remember the trip that Parsons and I took to Lucerne this winter? We met Horst and Wolfgang there. They sent us a beer at the guest house dining room. We had a good evening together, talking about Switzerland. Parsons invited them here to his wedding reception." I sounded overly apprehensive, talking too quickly, I knew, expecting the dangers of deeper troubles to come.

Follum asked the brothers, "Do you like Bad Issel? Have you been here before?"

Horst said, "Never. We had hoped to get a tour around with Bradford."

Follum said, "Tomorrow I can go around with you, too, show you some things Bradford doesn't know."

Horst smiled a victorious smile at me as he said, "Wolfgang and I would be delighted."

I said, "Eric means we can see the sights together."

"We know what Eric means."

Follum seemed puzzled, as if I was walking in a parallel world, a slight remove from his understanding. So much of evil went right over his head.

Callard, who had caught the scent of fresh adventure, sidled up to our group. He introduced himself to the brothers and asked where they were having dinner, after this happy reception.

Horst said, "We had hoped to be with Bradford and his friend, Eric, but we understand that is not possible."

I said, "Follum and I promised Katherine..."

Callard interrupted, being a quick study on matters of this kind, thankfully quick. He said, "Think no more about it, my Swiss friends. I personally will introduce you to the Krakow Klub, a crowd of lonely émigrés from the Polish motherland. Fabulous Polksa Keilbasa and wheat beer with lemon wedges. Camaraderie, layered with open welcome. Bradford and Follum will take their fussy Katherine elsewhere, I am sure, the three of them always shunning my simple, friendly sausages."

I said, "Thank you ever so much, Callard. Horst, the two of you are in good hands."

Horst looked unhappy, however, as I retreated with Follum. I hated hurting Horst and Wolfgang, our night still strong in my mind, they offering me their double love. But it was more important that I protect Follum. Callard's eyes followed us with a meaningful stare.

The *Sekt* had cooled enough for Frau Langenscheidt to open the bottles with pops and overflows, the paid hostess stepping up to her role, perhaps a bit guilty at the scarcity of the ice. She sliced the two-layer cake into small pieces, the porcelain figurines of a soldier and his bride sinking knee-deep inside the warm frosting, and she portioned the slices among the small plates.

Before we could leave, however, good manners said we must dance with Inga and pin a dollar bill or two on her dress, using the bracelet pincushion with dozens of pins on her wrist. I was first in line to dance, making awkward circles to the accordion music and finding a ten dollar bill for her sleeve at the end. Follum followed with his energetic Wisconsin version of a polka step and Inga overjoyed having a turn with an authentic dancer. Her cheeks grew pink with excitement. She was pretty in a thick way, her solid neck a match for her ankles, with a roses-and-cream complexion and damp pale hair. For a moment, I saw something of what Parsons must have seen.

He was standing alone by the table watching the progress of the money polka. I went over to him and said, "May I have this dance, Parsons? I'm out of large bills, though, but everybody will be astonished to see us circling around the floor."

"Thanks, anyway, Bradford. I'll wait here."

I said, "Callard is taking the Swiss brothers to the Krakow Klub, to introduce them to Polish hospitality."

"Callard's friends may be too airy-fairy for them."

"Somehow, I shouldn't think so."

"Good. I just want people to get along."

I felt a pang of remorse for Parsons, and Inga, as well. He was doing the dutiful act instead of a desired one. What love transpired between them could evaporate within the year, replaced with years of drudgery from a hasty choice? What strange pressures Parsons must have perceived and accepted to get married, merely for everybody to get along. Peace in my time. Like Woodrow Wilson, and I supposed the marriage had the same promise as his League of Nations.

# BRAHMS AROUND THE SHOULDER

> A lonely impulse of delight
> Drove to this tumult in the clouds.
> *— William Yeats*

MUSIK BECAME A THIRD LOVER that Follum and I took up without jealousy, a personage that we included in our days, sitting quietly at lunches with the occasional comment, coming forward as evenings fell. Follum loved Musik more than I, while I stood back, waiting my turn. We three were regulars at the modern music hall, the first building in Stuttgart up from the rubble.

Follum asked me to a July performance, three rarely-performed Bach cantatas in a single evening. It promised a nice change after my Beretta weekend. We took the streetcar down from Bad Issel, the sun still above the horizon as we entered the hall. Only the musical diehards would be there, the promise of a sticky, airless hall sure to turn away the faint-of-heart. Captain McQuire was in her season ticket place up front. Musik would not need his own seat, happy to be in standing room just behind us.

Our places were in the far back, but the hall's acoustics were perfect for this sort of performance, the birch-paneled concert shell behind the orchestra launching the sound deeply across the front tiers, giving it a fuller body as it went. The last rows, typically full, got the perfect sound, an oddly demotic arrangement for German architects. Perhaps it was a mistake that they discovered too late to rectify.

First was a secular cantata, one of those fancies that Bach wrote when spring burst over his cottage garden in Leipzig, perfume from the lilacs wafting through the open window of his study. The audience conversed in muffled tones, the concert hall as sacred as the cathedral. While the musicians and singers came quietly from either side of the stage, rustling on soft-soled shoes, the hall was nearly silent, then awash in applause as the conductor strode to the podium, a white-haired symbol of power. There was a minute of orchestral tuning and testing, then the tap of the baton.

The opening chorus assailed us with voices, horns, trumpets, oboes, drums, bells, a special row of pizzicato cellos and the entire orchestra, all singers at full-tilt from the first note, shouting the joy of warm winds and fields of green. It was such an outburst of sound that my eyes filled with tears, a spine-rippling, unsummoned ecstasy. On it went, as I took in a breath and felt there was no more air to take in. I looked over at Follum who was absorbing the music almost as a physical supper, rich sustenance from the one, two, three, one, two, three rhythm. It was a primeval cadence calling for the green men to emerge from the leafy shadows.

I saw Follum as the blessed son, favorite scion of an ancient tribe of musicians, dating back to centuries behind Bach when forests covered central Europe, music ascending slowly on the smoky sun-shafts between the trees. He was a golden man, clothed in the layers of chords and I was there only as a privileged outsider, an untutored spouse by chance let in on the clandestine ceremonies, from time beyond time. How was Bach so full of desire, physically lustful, that mere notes brought forth such an upwelling from the oldest part of the brain, the sexual part? How could mere music give me this sudden up-rush of pleasure, this unexpected erection? Bach and Follum merged into a single object of longing, flesh and idea one.

I reached over for his hand, closing mine slowly around his. He did not turn to look at me but returned my tight grasp as the chorus rose high above the wind instruments, trumpets calling us to the ideal nature there for the having, diminished sevenths engorging into the full bloom of tonic majors. Would I ever be as happy as this music, my lover and I riding along the upsurge into the clouds and to a clear sky above? As the first movement neared its end, the contrapuntals came together into a single note across ten octaves, voices and instruments growing and growing, stronger and higher, then fading from sight in barely perceptible steps as a boat leaving the shore, until there was finally nothing on the horizon. The hall had a stunned stillness before the sharp applause.

The next movements were more circumspect, soloists exploring the melodies given up so generously in the opening chorus, one on top of another. In the sixth part, the chorus rebuilt the first elation with more gravity, slower-paced but culminating with a finale so layered with sound that it seemed it could not possibly go higher, but higher and broader it went, voices upon voices, trumpets now grown to a battalion strong. If sunlight broke through in the opening chorus, it now burned the eyes like an exploding star. Was spring ever so happy to be here once again? Canny old Bach heard it all in his study, his ink-stained hand scratching the pen across paper as the new leaves in the church-yard turned green.

My hand loosened its grip on Follum's and slid away, passion spent. We walked outside to the cooler air, stood well away from the crowd and McQuire at the open doors. I told him,

"I didn't know that Bach could be so sensual. That final crescendo, going up and up, over on itself, up higher and higher."

Eric smiled as he said, "Did you get all hot and bothered, again?"

"Yes. How can an oratorio do that?"

"Lust. It's your most endearing quality."

"Is that bad?" I asked.

"No, I want us to have that every day. If I can just keep ahead of you a few steps, teasing you with Bach, tantalizing with a bit of Bizet, we have a great erotic chase ahead of us. I can't wait to see what you do with Bach's *Phoebus und Pan*."

"You're going to say that we already should have left for Tangier. I know."

"I'm not going to stop asking. One day we will walk right past the concert hall, across to the Bahnhof, calmly take the train to Marseilles, then a creaky boat over to the coast of Africa, and at last the short walk to our white-washed house on the edge of town. Desire and happiness mingled beside climbing roses and the aroma of a lamb tagine."

"Can Musik come with us?"

"If you want," he answered.

"I see him as the opposite of you, tall with jet-black dyed hair, severely cut, expressive long hands and an elegant slouch. He wears a linen suit with notes written all over it, Brahms around the shoulder, Mozart arias spiraling down around the knee, and Beethoven on the cuffs. He's quite different from either of us, in fact. He loves you but just smiles at me. I know that you see him sometimes when I'm not around."

"Is this the Bradford family madness you talk about?"

"I like to let go at times."

The bell rang for the second half and we were the last into our seats. Two short cantatas followed, not with the explosion of sound of the *Spring Cantata*. The final chorus of the evening exposed a glimmer of the first, voices merging into a vast single note, high above the busy violins and woodwinds. The percussion joined as the chorus spread into two notes, closer in tone to the orchestra, and then, finally, the theme was repeated with three notes, strong and intermingled with the elbowed energy of the full orchestra. I knew that my mind was free-wheeling, the music commingled with my shredded thoughts of love.

The Germans did not stint with their applause, bringing the full chorus and orchestra back for more bows, the conductor grumpier with each succeeding request. When it was time to go, Follum raised his eyebrows, looking down at my pants.

I said, "No, nothing this time, but I loved it anyway. Musik told me that he did, too."

# THE AFRICAN HOT

> My candle burns at both ends,
> it will not last the night.
> But, ah, my foes, and, oh, my friends,
> it gives a lovely light.
> *— Edna St. Vincent Millay*

"PLEASE DON'T GO OUT WITH him," Follum said.

"He asked me a couple of weeks ago. I can't just say no," I said.

"The way he looks at you."

"What way?"

"India man wants to have sex with you. I can tell. Do you want me to tell you how I know?"

"No. Why don't you come along, too?" I expected that Follum would not want to accompany Garinder Sagar and me to Indian Independence Day. It was scheduled on the big field of Killesberg Park, a celebration of the tenth anniversary of independence. Since August 15th fell on a Saturday, Garinder set it up for us to meet there at two in the afternoon, 1400 in Army parlance. It was still hot for a German midsummer, a stifling heat that started at dawn, up to well over a 100F by noon.

"He didn't invite *me*, did he?"

"I know, but it's hardly a personal picnic. Every Indian national in this part of Germany will be there. There will be fireworks and music. You would have a good time."

"No. Why don't you just call him and say no?"

"I can't Eric. Garinder would be hurt."

"I hate being jealous, but I am."

"Nothing will happen. I'm yours now, you're mine, Eric. We're lovers."

"Say it again; I like the sound of it."

Secret love was hard on both of us, immersed in the disapproving depths of the US Army. We had not been alone together for more than a few hours in the past month, a surreptitious touching of hands or a full body embrace in the shadows for a few seconds. The urgency was building.

I said, "We have the trip planned for September. A week on the French Riviera. I'll make it up to you then."

"But Callard will be there, too."

"You know that Callard always wants to go off on his own. We'll have plenty of time alone."

"I really need that. Are you sure he can find what he wants in Nice?"

"Every city in France has dope."

I hated making Follum unhappy, but his ability to be hurt so easily was one of his most disarming qualities. It was an odd part of a man with such startling Nordic good looks, tall and fair, with the broad hands of a farmer. I knew that Garinder held something more than simple friendship for me, but it would never get in the way of the bond with Follum. Our week in Paris had opened us up, made another life impossible.

I wanted to kiss Follum, to reassure him, but I affected my most manly clasp of the hand on his shoulder because Army eyes were watching from the windows of the schloss, I knew. He smiled weakly as I walked across the parade ground and out the front gate. I took the streetcar down the hill from Bad Issel, through the suburbs to the edge of the park. The streetcar was crowded with Swabian couples and families headed for a day of drinking at the Killesberg Biergartens. These were clustered around the brass band in the revolving central concert shell, and on this sweltering day every table would be filled.

The Hindu celebration was off to the side, a minor event at this spacious park, fields and landscaped woods to separate its various events. Women in saris with children, men in turbans were all heading in one direction. Every member of the Indian community in Stuttgart would be there; almost all were employees of Daimler-Benz and their families.

We had first met Garinder a month ago at one of the Bach Evenings at the concert hall, Follum and I drinking glasses of Riesling at the interval, a small table in the far corner. Garinder came across with his own glass and asked if he could join us.

"I thought Americans only drank beer," he said. His English was perfect.

"I would say, Eric, that this man went to school in Kansas or somewhere in the Midwest."

"A good ear, Henry Higgins, it was University of Indiana. My name is Garinder Sagar, from Bombay." He was darker skinned than other Indians I had met, dressed in a well-tailored black suit, a paisley tie, English shoes.

I introduced myself and Follum and identified us as Bach-lovers.

"American Bach-lovers so far from the heartland."

"We hunt everywhere for the perfect performance." I could see Garinder liked banter.

"A merry chase."

I asked, "Do you live in Stuttgart, or are you a visitor?"

"I'm assigned with the Indian consulate here, looking after

the needs of our growing numbers here. India asks Germany for engineering and manufacturing know-how."

"You're an industrial spy, then?"

"Nothing so grand. Everything above board."

"You live at the consulate?"

"No, on my own, in an apartment near the consulate. Right over there." He pointed across the Konzerthallepark to a row of villas that had survived the allied bombings, 19th Century merchants' houses with gardens and high iron fences. I knew that most of them had been converted to consuls and foreign emissary offices. The Villa Ingrid was on the street behind.

Follum asked, "So you like Bach, too?"

He said, "I studied Bach at Indiana. A music major, would you believe?"

"Do you play an instrument?"

"Not well."

We talked about life in Stuttgart, mostly asking Garinder about his life, where he went at night, restaurants that he liked, trips nearby he had taken. He relished the talk about himself, his family back in Bombay, his sister who was studying to be a concert cellist, his older brothers who would take over the family exporting business, spices and seeds. Foreign Service was for him, however, what the youngest son was expected to do.

His candor and openness were appealing in this Germany, where everybody held secret cards so close to the chest. Follum and I were trained not to provide anything, so Garinder got little information in return. He was polite enough to not ask a direct question, but waited for us to offer anything. We did not.

As the bell rang the second half of the concert, Garinder asked, "Will you be here next week, for the Brahms? Perhaps I can take the two of you to dinner afterwards? I enjoy using my English and being with non-Germans."

I looked at Follum and he nodded. I said, "Yes, we'll meet you here next Saturday at the intermission."

"Splendid. I will look forward to my mysterious music-loving friends." Our lack of informative talk had not gone unnoticed, and I supposed that he already suspected we were from Schloss Issel. There were Americans living in Stuttgart, but only Schloss Issel held quantities of university men, the kind who sought out the concert hall.

A week later after the concert, Follum and I had dinner with Garinder at a restaurant in walking distance from the hall, another evening of one-way flow of information. I had already sensed that Follum was nervous as I enthusiastically questioned about Calcutta and the Himalayas, and Garinder was quick with lengthy replies. He promised to send me a book about India after the end of the British. Follum said very little.

As we left the restaurant, Garinder asked, "Can my elusive new friends give me their mail address, their music-filled cottage in the woods? Where I can send the book?" He smiled at me, knowing it was a chess move.

I said, "Better yet, we'll met you here next Saturday, take *you* to dinner. No need to pay lots of postage." Check-mate avoided.

He said, "But it's the Debussy and Ravel evening, not my special favorites."

"Nonsense, you need the mists of the Paris as well as the straightforwardness of the Germans."

"Very well. Next Saturday."

As Follum and I walked to the streetcar stop, I looked back to see if Garinder observed us getting on the Bad Issel car. I could not see if anyone watched.

Follum said, "I don't like him."

"Why not?"

"He only looks at you when we're talking. He has a hard-on for you."

"A Hindu admirer, with peeled grapes and emeralds."

"Don't make fun of me. I really don't like him."

"I'm sorry, Eric. He's making a special effort to buy the

book about India. I'll go to the intermission next week and tell him that we can't see him anymore."

"Why not just forget about him? I feel him horning in between us."

"Because we have few enough in Germany being nice to us. I think we should back out with honor and good manners."

He said, "I need to keep you near where I can love you."

"I love you, too. You know that."

"When I was a boy on the farm, I used to hold eggs so hard they would crack open. I couldn't help it. I know that I am doing that to you."

"It's not a problem, Eric." Was it a problem? I was not sure.

During that following week, Captain Mcquire asked me to represent the Historical Section at the monthly Visitor's Day, local officials and businessmen receiving a short tour of Schloss Issel. We had a small room of the Central Registry open and an office full of analysts for non-sensitive programs for the visitors, then a short walk over to the officers club for tea, sherry and sandwiches. Colonel Rosscommon gave the group a speech, a short and vague description of our mission, his dress uniform more impressive to the Germans than his words. The visitors were then accompanied with arms around their shoulders, new friends we said, to the front gate. The secrets of the schloss would still be safe.

There were thirty in this month's group, each with a name-tag identifying their organization and we enlisted aides were asked to act like sheep dogs, blocking any strays that looked down the halls to the more sensitive offices. Garinder appeared out of the group and walked up to me, noticing my sewed on name-tag. His own name-tag said *Indian Charge d'Affaires*.

"How handsome you look in uniform, Bradford."

"Discovered at last."

"And I thought it was just the music that brought you to Germany."

"You can understand why I did not talk about it."

"Not really."

"I guess we're on for the Debussy this weekend?"

"I can't wait. Dinner afterwards?"

"Of course."

Follum did not want to go. I said I would try to get out of dinner, be back early and wake him when I got in. That was the night that Garinder invited me to the Independence Day celebration. He said he would bring the colored powders, a spread for the lawn and a hamper with sandwiches. We did not mention Follum at all that evening and I did not wake him when I returned late.

As I walked through the Killesberg birch trees towards the gathering of Indians, I could smell the strong perfumes of those before me on the walk, flower scents mixed with spices and musk.

Garinder was already there, lying on one elbow upon a cotton spread with red and green flowers, a wicker hamper and a crescent of pillows arranged to face the musicians. I wondered if a servant or two, several castes lower, had tended to all this, reserving the shade from the small tree since early morning, merging without a word into the citizenry as I arrived. Garinder wore all white, a loose shirt with a tab collar and trousers, and an over-sized turban, wrapped into a major Brahmin statement

I said, "Now who wears the handsome uniform?"

He stood up to shake my hand. "My mother's people, the Garinders, come from Rajasthan. Men are naked there without a turban."

"You must show me how to tie one."

"Gladly. Please sit down, the music is about to begin."

Two sitars began a raga, a very old one, Garinder told me. It was the raga that welcomed in midsummer in the centuries before the British; it would go on for seven hours, telling a long story of gods and goddesses.

Seven hours, my lord.

I said, "You were lucky to get a place in the shade."

Garinder just smiled. He said, "I have read that this hot weather is a sort of *Uber-Foehn* coming all the way from the Sahara, across the Alps and slithering down into Germany. Usually there is strong wind, but this one is still. They call it the *Afrikanischer Heiss*, but it's much the same as the hot, dry days before the monsoons at home."

"Are any of your family in Germany?"

"No. We will talk later, but now we must sit against the pillows and listen."

The raga from the sitar was slow, with spronging and twanging sounds between the more sharply picked ones. I listened intently for a half hour or so, looking without success for design in the strange music. The raga beguiled, beckoned to give in to its patterns, to submit to its insistence. Two more sitar players arrived with their instruments, and then, after a short while, three more, then three more. The sound grew much more complex, one rank of sitars playing insistent, repetitive notes up and down, while another group played a high melody above the cadence like clouds above the earth.

Even more sitars and their players arrived, adding another register above the seemingly already complete one. Where there any sitars left in India? I felt drugged and exhilarated at the same time, the music an elixir, faster and faster, a dozen rhythms beating against each other and coming into conjunction just often enough to make you imagine that you saw a plan in the greater disorder.

I had not noticed when Garinder had placed his hand on my forearm, well into the ascent of the raga. I was aware I had given in, supplicated myself to personal closeness in the acoustical high. Logical thought was difficult, but I summoned up the idea that two men on an Indian blanket, holding hands in the brew of heat and this now ravishing raga, was a very strange thing. How was it that I was part of this, like a single American whooping crane in the midst of an extended flock of elegant Asiatic cranes?

The late arrivals among the Indian nationals walked over to Garinder's blanket and bowed slightly with palms upright together. His high rank was obvious to all except me. They took no notice of my presence, as if I were merely one of the pillows that supported him. Had there been many pillows before me? My face was shiny with perspiration, my shirt damp across the front, but I could feel Garinder's hand cool on my arm and his face showed no effects of the heat.

What a strange afternoon, I thought, as the sun finally went below the horizon and the sky darkened. Time was suspended or expanded, I could not figure out which. An hour spread out into two more, and then it was entirely dark. The music was dense and threatening by now, as if thorny shrubs had grown up around us. My mind had been sucked dry of thought and filled with sound. The sitars stopped suddenly on a single note and the silence almost hurt the ears. Garinder stood up and I did, too, trying to not stumble as I did. He pulled an orange scarf from his pocket and waved it. From beyond the rows of sitars the fireworks exploded into large chrysanthemums while whining circular rockets made a forest of uprights between them. After twenty minutes, it was over.

The sitars then began an anthem of sorts, more melodic, different from the raga, and all the people sang. A national anthem, I supposed. Afterwards, we sat and ate the sandwiches, mostly in silence. The other Indians threw colored powders at each other, laughing and the children yelling, but nobody came near the blanket of the *chargé d'affaires* and his friend. We remained colorless. Garinder asked if I wanted to stay at his flat that night, Bad Issel so far away in the dark, but I explained that a soldier needed to sleep in his own quarters.

"A soldier? How amusing."

"The summer streetcars run until well after midnight. Thank you anyway."

"You'll be safe, then?"

"I'm sure. I think the raga exhausted my emotions."

"That's what it is designed to do. To make you pliant and suggestive."

"It worked, but the docile soldier still must go back."

"Pity, but we have another anniversary next year. All of India knows how to wait for what it wants."

Nothing happened between Garinder and me that night, except my new awareness that I had the opportunity for sensual adventure should I choose to explore it. Stuttgart harbored many hidden resources for a young man, especially one like me. I was aware that Garinder and I shared a delight in verbal combat, teasing the opponent with words that implied more than action would allow. It was fun to flirt with a forward burst, then retreat if the foe struck too close. Follum did not know how to play that game, since he was uncomplicated and loyal. Should I feel guilty that I savored the parry and thrust, the teasing, the shadow play? Probably so, but once you knew how to swim it was difficult stay on the shore to please your friends who could not.

Years later in Santa Fe I would meet an earnest young man who claimed that he flew each night over oceans and mountains to India, had another life there and then flew back west at sunrise in time to take up his job as a dishwasher at the five star hotel. My friends laughed at such absurdity, but I was one of the few who believed him and wondered if the marigold he customarily wore in his buttonhole had germinated beside the Ganges.

# Narcissus

I believe we should all behave quite
differently if we lived in a warm,
sunny climate all the time.
— *Noel Coward*


CALLARD CAME SOUTH WITH US,
and announced he would disappear as he had in Paris into a
poppy heaven, somewhere in the back streets of Old Nice. This
time he had his own money from endeavors around the Bad
Issel fountain. He was the perfect third wheel, seldom around to
make awkward silences, and he did most of the driving down to
the coast.

We booked into a small hotel two streets back from the
front. Next morning at breakfast on the shady terrace, Madame
served us her sliced black figs, covered with *crème anglaise*, a slice
of cheese, black bread and a single cup of strong black coffee. She
cut across my request with, "No, the café au lait is not possible.
You boys must learn the ways *niçoises*."

As Callard wolfed down his figs and got up to leave,
downing his coffee in a gulp, I asked him, "Where will you be if
we need you?"

"You won't need me. Best you don't know where."

"Are you sure that there is a place in Nice?"

"Every French town has one. A gift from the colonies." He tied a kerchief around his neck, adjusted the beret to an exact angle. Somehow, he transmogrified himself from the sturdy Polish peasant so invisible to authorities on the back lanes of Stuttgart to a slimmer French version, a rake out on the town, cigarette perfectly slanted from his lips. Invisibility restored.

"And how can you recognize it? A green door?" I asked.

"I'll tell you when you're a little bit older."

We watched him as he sauntered to the corner, turned to wave back, because he knew we would be watching his loping gait, and he evaporated into the side street. Only once, back in Bad Issel did I try to follow Callard, eager to practice my surveillance talents, but he was immediately difficult to keep up with, melding into small groups, sitting down, then standing up to go off in a new direction, turning into another person as if his foot-prints modified into paw-prints, then into the sharp angles of bird-tracks, and off the ground entirely into the darkness beyond. This time he merely rounded a corner, but I knew if I ran to look, the street would be empty.

From that first breakfast, Madame sensed the desire between Follum and me and fell into the role of compliant chambermaid, as if we were players in an opera. She was nosy, but not mean or disapproving. She brought an extra down pillow to the room that night and a tray with almond-butter cookies and glasses of a sweet, ochre-colored liqueur. She said, "Is the bed soft enough for you? As if you would care. Already the Côte d'Azur makes its mark. Good boys."

The upper branches of the fig tree gently stroked the closed shutters of our room each night, not at all disturbing but sensual in the night breeze. It xylophoned us to sleep with its foliage-muted ratta-tatta-tat, ratta-tatta-tat.

Follum and I spent the daylight hours on the beach beside

the Promenade, a narrow strip of pebbles and wood-slatted beach chairs rented by the hour, towels for a few francs more. The water was pleasant enough, still warm from a summer baking under the sun, clear and greenish blue, the horizon blending into the sky. One day followed another with perfect warm sunlight, a pale sauterne in this late September, the fall storms holding back.

As we drove through the towns along the coast, Villefranche, Cannes, Juans-les-Pins, we could see that the occupants of Mercedes sedans, even our battered relic with the crystal vases, were not popular with the French. I noticed the shaken fists and spitting as we passed, years of pent-up hate too strong to ignore, but when they became aware we were merely Americans in a German car, their anger cooled. Several asked what was wrong with a Peugeot or a Reynard; we must get a proper French car for a French holiday. Set fire to that devil, one woman said.

Nursing our sunburns on the fourth morning, Follum drove while I navigated us westwards along the coast and up the inland road to Grasse. Follum had read that the small church on the market place housed a famous French organ, a three-manual instrument, pipes cast from the meltdown of captured Prussian cannons, panels of oak from Normandy, beech pedals from the Île de France. A local nobleman commissioned it from the genius Cavaillé-Coll, and it was a romantic, modern instrument unlike anything stiff and military that might be shipped across the Rhine.

We found a parking space near the church, *l'eglise de Saint Eustache.* It was a low structure spanning the narrow end of the market square, all but hidden behind a line of horse-chestnuts. Stuccoed a butter yellow in the past, the church was now diminished to a paler shade, chunks fallen away to expose the sandstone blocks underneath. A bell in a wrought-iron framework topped the stone tower to the side of the entry.

Follum said, "It's a famous little church. Before the war, people came just to hear the organ, a smaller, sweeter version of the one we heard in Paris. Modern music played on a French organ."

"Will they let you play it?"

"I'm hoping so. Let's ask."

A young prelate with pimples disappeared into the bowels behind the altar and produced the organist, a small, older man with half-glasses. He spoke English mixed with the soft, slow French of the south and his name was Père Lavalle.

"You wish to play our organ?" he said, as he looked at Follum over his glasses.

"If you please, Father. I studied at St. Olaf in the States."

"Ah, I have heard of St. Olaf. What will you play on such an organ as ours?

"I know a Franck chorale and some Bach, but I can sight-read anything you prefer."

"*Alors*, I have a Guilmant sonata now on the music stand, not a difficult piece. Nineteenth Century. Let's test you out."

As we walked up to the organ balcony, I asked Follum, "Do you need me to work the bellows?"

"Nobody pumps anymore. It will surely be electrified."

Lavalle asked, "Shall I turn for you?"

"Please, Father."

I took a chair at the side of the gallery as the testing procedure began. Follum clicked on the light, turned a switch marked *soufflage*, studied the sheet music on the stand, pulled out several stops, checked below him for the foot-pedals, and adjusted the bench. He sat with his back to the church below, the ornate façade of the organ looming above. Lavalle stood to his right, noting with approval Follum's familiarity with the starting-up protocol, waiting to turn the pages.

The sound filled the small church, bright and without echo from the close plaster walls. Follum played the music without looking down at the keyboards or the foot-pedals, and, if the local organist was not impressed, I was. Pulling out other stops for the flute and horns, he filled out the rumbling, below-the-earth sound with the sharp notes from the treble. Lavalle turned the page each time Follum nodded, smoothing his hand across the sheet with a quick deftness. I had an initial worry that Follum would falter, play a wrong note to a derisive sneer from the old man, but he sailed high above the French Nineteenth Century, unafraid of the murky progressions and Parisian dissonances.

I looked up at the rows of pewter-colored pipes which produced this sound. A central rank stood out in front of the rest and was topped by a Byzantine dome, a metal sea-bird with outstretched wings as its finial. Two side ranks had smaller domes, swagged up to the center with the expert foldings of pewter ribbons. Aristide Cavaillé-Coll was a Frenchman at heart, unable to resist a bit of ornament in his utility.

It was ten minutes later when Lavalle turned the last page and sat down to listen to the rest of the sonata. I wondered if there was a competitive spirit operating here, Follum proving more adept than the priest, the long-caped specter of jealousy sidling out from the wings, eyes narrowed. But the old man appeared genuinely pleased to find a fellow expert. He stood to pat Follum on the shoulder, as if he had found his own son again.

"*Eh, bien.* Do not run through Guilmant, my boy, stride through. What agile fingers you have, strong hands. Good feet."

"We studied mostly the Germans at St. Olaf. Very few French, I'm afraid. I like this piece."

"Guilmant has come back, almost forgotten even here in his own France."

"May I play a Bach prelude for you, Father?"

Lavalle waved an assent with his hand and sat down in the other chair; Follum adjusted the stops and took off. Unlike his attentive rendition of the French composer, Follum rocked slightly back and forth to the Bach, happy to be in the familiar land of Prelude and Fugue, first voice followed smartly by second voice. It was a known world. If Guilmant used the forest shadows and bands of mist as his handmaidens, Bach stood alone on an open meadow in the noonday sun, bright, clear, and unequivocal.

Lavalle asked what brought Follum and me to *Saint Eustache*, a forgotten niche at the side of the world. Follum explained that we were American military, on a week's holiday. He had read in the Herald Tribune about the Cavaillé-Coll organ here, wanted to play it because it would not be so grand nor so intimidating as its siblings in Copenhagen and Paris.

The old man said, "You must return, then, be part of us. *Malheureusement*, I am old, fingers stiffened, memory not so quick. We held Wednesday concerts here when I was in my prime, visitors from all of France, as well as the weekly music for the mass. With a new young man here, our flock would grow. If they do not come for the Lord, they will for the organ, music in the air again. We can reconstitute the old string quartet and bring back *les vieillards* who can make it up the steps to the gallery. Are you Catholic?"

"Lutheran."

"No matter, men of all water are at the keyboard now. I understand there is an atheist in Montpellier playing our beloved Reboulot."

"I will think about it, Father."

"Don't expect the pay to be good. A few francs only, and, naturally, the glory of God. There is a separate house reserved only for the organist."

"I won't expect good pay."

"Bach is not so popular here as in St. Olaf. You must study the great French composers. Vierne and Langlais, both blind. I will give you a list of the others. You will be busy."

We walked out of the church and took a table outside at the café near where we parked. I could tell that Follum was delighted to be so appreciated, to be asked. When we fantasized about going off together, living in illicit foreignness, it was always me as the famous one, the painter yet to be. Here, he would be the celebrated musician, locally beloved, the pride of *Saint Eustache*, while I painted my Mannerist landscapes on daily jaunts to the country. It pleased me to imagine that the pressure would be off me to be the Illustrious Painter. I could be merely the man that shares the bed of the organist, *le virtuose de Grasse*, makes his nights happy.

He said, "Katherine was right on the mark. The South of France instead of Tangier, but only after we get properly discharged. Legally, not runaways."

I said, "The water will be safe to drink here and the food better. It was more fun when we were suspected felons, however, lurking in the Kasbah, wearing our gallabiyas, smearing our faces with camel-dung, keeping an eye out for the prison ship."

"You've grown bold and light-hearted about Morocco, now that we aren't going there."

"Wishy-washy Bradford they called me in school. Not entirely undeserved."

"Maybe Katherine can come here, too. We'll rent her a room in the organist's house."

I said, "If we waive army transportation home, we can get out of the service over here in Europe. Your release is in March, and I can meet you here in May. You'll have three months with Père Lavalle, practicing away at his list."

Follum and I both considered the idea, drinking our coffee. Was it truly possible for us to live in France? Could I make a living at art? Could I borrow enough from the family back in Middleton, if only for a year? We would not survive only on Follum's few francs from the church, and certainly not on the Glory of God. There was much to think about.

I recognized that the roles Follum and I played with each other were reversing. If he was gaining strength, was I losing a similar amount of strength? It did not seem so, and I considered the possibility of a meeting of equals, partners on the same footing. Maybe not so bad. Perhaps the best arrangement is where the one evolves, while the other waits, then the reverse, then the reverse of that again. I recalled a dream I had after Callard and I returned from Berlin. Male dancers clad in white suits with black stripes, in the swirling mist, coming forward into focus, then receding into the curlicues of fog, one at a time. Was this what Follum and I would become?

Callard had not resurfaced by the next morning and we needed to start the twelve-hour drive back to Bad Issel. I wondered if he had run into foul play. Madame served our plates of figs, swimming deep in *crème anglaise*, a special treat for my brave soldiers, she said. The coffee was so strong it belonged in a fountain pen.

"Madame, do you remember our friend, Callard, who checked in with us?"

"The opium fiend?"

I checked my urge to lash out. "Yes. Do you know where he might be?"

"All of Nice knows. I will write down the address, a narrow street above the fish market."

Madame hugged us both, gave us a handful of early narcissus, forced especially for her in the greenhouses of Menton; stems cut short, they went nicely into the bud-vases. Follum drove around the market twice before we spotted the small street up the hill, Rue Victor Hugo. While he waited with the motor running, I knocked. A young, attractive woman opened the door, in fact, painted an apple green. We were looking for our friend, Callard. Could he be here?

"*Mais, oui.* Follow."

In the back room the haze was honey-laden, smoky like an East Texas barbecue shack, and the patrons were lying on their sides, covered with tasseled shawls. I peered down at several before I found Callard, fully dressed, smelling of sweat. His dilated blue eyes, almost black, gave him the startled look of a deer, ready to bolt. To placate him, keep him from running, I helped him up to a sitting position and sat beside him. I kept my arm around his shoulder and placed his flattened beret, now devoid of chic, back on his head. His natty scarf was nowhere in view.

I said, "Time to go. Back to Bad Issel."

"I seem to have lost track. Have you had fun without me?"

"Loads. Follum has the engine running."

"What a smart fellow he is."

"On the way home, we'll tell you about our day in Grasse."

"Oh, good, a day in Grasse." The matrix of his world was coming back, pieces here and there, nothing solid yet.

"Why is your face that ghastly color?" he asked.

"Sunburn, Callard."

In the daylight he looked wasted, eyes swollen with dark half-moons, his reddish-blond hair matted and dank. He had been so untouched by the dope in Paris, almost elated by it; I wondered if this was an inferior strain in the south, stronger, more damaging, perhaps a cheaper sort from the *Indochine*. He opened the back door and lay down, pulling up the tartan wool lap-robe to his chin, looking for all the world like a ruined Scottish princess on the way back to the castle.

As we drove away, he said, "No more *crème anglaise* for Callard," and fell right to sleep without so much as a wheeze. The scent of the newly-cut narcissus filled the car.

The snow began to fall as we drove along Lake Annecy, heavier on the way through the Savoy to Switzerland. We skirted Geneva, went over the mountains and down into our Bad Issel, where the storm had already stopped and a full moon glittered on the granular thin carpet of new snow. It was good to be back safely in the land of Bach, where strict order reigned and strange ideas seldom took root.

# Blue Light

On must not put a loaded rifle on the stage
if no one is thinking of firing it.
— *Anton Chekhov*

IT WAS A GRAY SATURDAY
afternoon when Captain McQuire made good on her offer to
include me in a sharp-shooter sortie. I was in my quarters reading
on the bed, barely enough power from the overhead bulbs to
see my bootleg copy of the still-banned *Lady Chatterley's Lover*, a
chance discovery at a kiosk along the Seine. A brisk knock and
Sergeant-Major Tetley walked right in.

"Herself wants you in the Orderly Room, Bradford. Now.
Civilian clothes, no ID."

"Can't you say I was out on the town?"

"You're not, are you?" He advised me to be smart about it,
Captain McQuire was sitting in his comfortable chair, tapping
her foot.

There was not a full selection of clothing in my locker. My
trusty, checkered sports jacket; the last of the white, button-down

shirts from Brooks Brothers; dark trousers; and black, cap-toe oxfords. No hat. No overcoat, because it was not cold outside. When I wore the same outfit for a night out with Callard, he said that I was a walking advertisement for the Shaker Heights Goodwill.

I pulled the cards with photos out of my wallet, but kept the Deutsch Marks. No military money, either. I knew this meant whatever we were doing was illegal, officially frowned upon, but from somewhere on high, required.

Callard was already there, in his German-student ensemble, beret pulled flat across the eyebrows, and perfectly round, tinted-lens glasses with black plastic rims. He was the perfect bomb thrower from Heidelberg, a dog-eared *Magister Ludi* in his pocket. McQuire wore a black, mid-length skirt, gray shirt with a man's black tie, dark raincoat. On her head, she angled a dark green Bavarian hat with a partridge tail-feather. She was indistinguishable from the mid-level clerks in the basement of the town hall. They both inspected my clothes, up and down, looking quickly away. Details in the car, McQuire said.

That was the usual Chevrolet sedan, no official numbers anywhere with a neutral license plate, waiting with the engine running. The driver was the young Sergeant Terrence that McQuire favored from the Motor Pool, born near her home town. Why she continued to select Callard and me was an enigma, with a full roster of career soldiers like Terrence to cast her dramas.

Callard said, when he and I approached the subject one night at the Bierstube Langenscheidt, that she trusted her boys to respond smartly and be more attentive to all manner of danger around them. You draftees are light on your feet, she said, dancing with verve around danger

I said, "It still seems odd why she chooses us."

"I know why. She as much as told me in one of our morning sessions."

"I like those mornings. She's as good as a real therapist."

Callard looked pained. "How would you know what real therapy was?"

"Okay, what did she say?"

"She told me that back home her younger brother was artistic, sensitive, not a lot different from me."

"A faggot, then?"

"She didn't use those words, but her meaning was clear. Her mother nagged the brother to become more manly, go deer hunting with the uncles, go out for football. He hated blood sports, but he was as strong-willed as the rest of the family, fought her every inch. The mother berated him at the dinner table with *Please pass the pansy a little more gravy*. She said the family tree had never before produced such fruit, that he was a mutant, maybe switched with another sickly infant at the hospital. It was disgraceful, unacceptable. Despite it all, he seemed to be making a place for himself. Then, as he was coming into his late teens, one night he hanged himself in the basement. McQuire never forgave her mother. It was part of what made her want to be a soldier, get away from Kansas."

I wondered if Sergeant Terrence, our driver, another All-American farm boy, knew that story, as we sped east along the autobahn. The captain said, "An East German professor of biology, Doktor Killesman, known for cooking up extraordinary liquids for the Soviet Army, will escape from an East-West scientific conference in Ulm. It will be good for our propaganda, a high-level defection."

Callard said, "We don't have to kill him, do we?"

"No, no, we *want* him to escape. A pre-arranged taxi will take him to the small local airport and an unmarked plane over to France."

"So he can make his microbes for Allies."

"Not for us to judge. Defectors are good for us, evidence that the enemy has morale problems, bad living conditions. We'll engineer any defection: ballet dancers, minor officials, poets, painters, professors. A new, happy life in the West."

He said, "So...why are we involved?"

"Traffic control. We'll shoot out the tires of any cars that try to follow; it will cause a traffic jam. The limestone bullets in our take-down Berettas, Fivolli silencers. They are in the trunk in clarinet cases."

I asked, "Where will this all happen?"

"Callard and I will be next to the church where we have a man waiting; he's already opened the windows in a room over the cafe. Bradford, you'll be across from us in the hotel room that we rented a week ago, clear shot of the narrows. The only way to the airport is through the cathedral square."

Callard asked, "Will other snipers be there?"

"Oh, yes, I almost forgot, six others from the Ulm field-office, but high command much prefers the Schloss Issel wrecking squad. They expect us to make it happen."

I said, "It sounds like our dove season back in Middleton, nine men shooting at the same small bird."

She said, "And a final word, the taxi with the defecting professor will have a blinking blue light. He will arrive in front of the Munster at sixteen hundred exactly. The tires of all the cars that follow need to be shot out, without exception."

From my second floor window, I could see McQuire, Bavarian hat still on, and Callard in the windows across the street. They could have been a Swabian brother and sister admiring the treasured façade of the Munster. I assembled the Beretta rifle from the sections cushioned in the case, each twist making a satisfying click. The rifle had a grip for the window sill, and a light-enhanced sight, clear cross-hairs at three hundred yards. It was an angle shot for me, down the street in front of the church. For a test, I focused in on a pigeon's eye, blinking nervously as if he knew I was watching him.

At ten minutes to the hour, the bronze doors to the church opened wide, organ music reverberated out into the square and the parishioners, voices raised in plainsong, streamed out by the dozens. Choir boys held aloft a saint's chair on their shoulders, the carved, wooden effigy rocking back and forth. More citizens poured forth with flags, banners and high crosses of colored glass. By our target time of 1600 hours, several hundred of the faithful had swarmed across and intermingled with the motor traffic in the square, reverently walking in the direction from where the professor's taxi was due. In minutes, the cathedral square was crammed with chanting and laughing citizens.

There would be no Traffic Control tonight. Had headquarters ever thought to consult a liturgical calendar? I could see a frantic McQuire, feather bobbing up and down, sending me the "T' signal, the universal order to stand down.

I took apart the rifle, returned each section to its velvet valley in the case. To rejoin the others across the square, I elbowed through the crowd near the multi-colored saint's chair, high in the middle of the street. It was the blessed St. James of Ulm, patron of the stained-glass window workers, on his festival outing.

On the way back to Schloss Issel, McQuire said, "Bradford, before our next mission, let's get you another sports jacket. That Harris tweed has had enough outings by now." I could not see Callard's face as he continued to look out the window at the farm lights in the countryside, but I was sure that he was smiling.

Professor Killesman got away, despite us. Perhaps headquarters in fact knew of the saintly procession, deemed it a smoke screen of sorts. The pursuing entourage became mired in the crowd as the taxi driver, chosen for his adeptness, honked his way through the faithful, blue light flashing. With his terrible formulas in his satchel, the good doctor arrived safely at the Ulm airport for his connecting flight to Paris.

# Hindu Rope Trick

Life is a glorious cycle of song
a medley of extemporanea,
and love is a thing that can never go wrong,
and I am Marie of Roumania
*— Dorothy Parker*

KATHERINE SAT ON THE EDGE of my desk with a dossier in her hand. She pulled out from the folder a group of papers stapled to photographs and placed them in front of me.

"These came out of the Vienna pouch, one of the Czech double-agents. He microfilmed the newest dossiers at the Prague KGB detachment, left the film taped under a bench in the Prater. It's been a week in processing, and the translators have just finished. What do you think?"

*Subject:* **Garinder Sagar**, *Charge d'Affaires, Indian Consulate, Stuttgart. Suspected of industrial espionage: theft of supercritical gas centrifuge for India's clandestine nuclear program.*

*Agent followed subject for appointments with other foreign consuls (Spanish, Turkish, Italian), and meetings with DeGussa AG (developed centrifuge in 1943)*

*15 August 57 at India Independence Day celebration, Killesberg Park, agent in adjoining woodland photographed subject with an unidentified man, possibly American (in dark glasses) (See attached photographs). Could be involved in theft.*

*Possible sexual misconduct. Request surveillance funds.*

"That's a bit scary, Katherine."

"I can shred it or reclassify it. Nobody in this office will know if I stamp it as Eyes Only."

"It was totally innocent."

"I know, but it looks bad. I recognized you in the grainy photo and I remember your telling me about Garinder."

"It's me, but no security issues were involved, I assure you."

"I know that, my dear, loyalty is not the issue. I was afraid it might cross Follum's desk. It's on his list of agents."

One of the photographs clearly showed Garinder's hand on my arm, his face turned with a smile, leaning down as if to kiss. Even in the fuzziness of the telephoto shot, Garinder was very photogenic. It would, however, be difficult, if not impossible, to explain to Follum.

I said, "It is against regulations to interfere, Katherine. Let's just leave it to the gods."

"They have evil senses of humor."

"So be it. I will tell Follum what to expect and try to explain."

She said, "Brave of you. The honorable way, but I have grave doubts."

I did talk to Follum. It was midweek, and we went to the Bierstube after work. Follum was being discharged in a few days, taking up Père Lavalle's offer as the organist in Grasse. We talked about that and other subjects for a while, then I put my hand on his arm, said I had something important to tell him.

"There is a photograph of me at the Killesberg picnic. You remember my talking about it?"

"The one with India man that I asked you not to go to?"

"Yes. I should have listened. It looks as if he and I are about to kiss. But nothing of the sort happened."

He waited a long time before commenting. "Then why does it look that way?"

"We were just talking, it was hot."

"Who took the photo?"

"A Czechoslovakian double agent. Katherine spotted it in the weekly pouch from Vienna. It will probably come across your desk tomorrow."

"Are you in danger?"

"Perhaps."

Follum asked me to give him time to think about it. I had hoped he would just push it aside, say he loved me just as much as ever, that he trusted me. He was unusually silent as we walked back to our quarters.

At breakfast the next morning, he joined my table.

He said, "I didn't get much sleep."

"I'm sorry, Eric."

"My love is complete and deep, but all the while you seem to play with me. I don't think you can help it. I thought if we had our year in Tangier or Grasse, away from the world, you might change. We could put a polish on love, make it better. But, now I know you won't change. You will always be looking over my shoulder at someone else. There will be other photographs, other India men, other excuses."

I said, "I'm more social than you, want to talk to others. That doesn't mean I would act on anything I said."

"It hurts too much, Harold. I can't do it. I can't trust a life with you in Grasse, knowing it could fall apart, leave me stranded."

"But you *can* trust me."

"No, I can't. I'm going to personnel today and change my discharge request, go home with Army transportation, go back to St. Olaf. Even if I have to pay for it myself."

"Is there nothing I can do?"

"No."

His handsome face was so distressed. There were no tears, but every other hint of sadness. I hated that I could bring that to him, to make such a wound. I knew that he was right. I could never be the faithful spouse he wanted, even if it was only a teasing glance at someone else or a game of seductive words. It was as part of me as my eyes.

I put my hand on his arm and asked, "Can we have one more night together?"

"I don't think so."

"I'm so ashamed, Eric. You are a beautiful man."

He avoided me for the rest of the week. I could see him going to an earlier breakfast, staying in his room instead of meeting the others at the Bierstube after work. At the Historical Section, he was deep into his dossiers. I was never aware that the photos with Garinder actually came to his desk. Katherine may have quietly arranged for their disappearance, shredded with the daily dispatches.

From the casement windows in the Section, I watched the car that took him to Frankfurt and the Army airplane back stateside, the sedan going down the hill between the grapevines, hopeful with their first green buds. I thought he looked up at the window, knowing I was watching, but I could not be sure. I wished that I could shed tears, but they did not come; instead, I felt a constricting force, almost a smothering, forcing me to take small breaths.

Katherine came over to me, put her hand on my shoulder.

She said, "Maybe he will change his mind."

"I don't think so. It seems as if nothing ever happened

between us, a great eraser just finished its work. He will marry Melanie the minute he gets back home, scour me out of his thoughts with some Nordic cleanser, have blond babies."

"You don't know that for sure."

"You were right to question. It didn't work, but I'm not sure I could have done anything else."

"What will you do now?"

"Art school, where I should have gone in the first place."

"That sounds right."

We both kept looking where the sedan had disappeared beyond the vineyards.

She said, "I have some news, as well, Harold."

She was resigning to go back to Vienna, to take care of her ailing mother-in-law, the dowager countess. They might open up the country house, shuttered since the war, no doubt in poor repair, and lease out the more desirable flat in Vienna for income.

I said, "I will say again, that you must call if there is ever need. I don't want you to lack any more."

She said, "You don't have enough to share and art school will cost money."

"There is always some extra for you."

"It would have been fun with you two in the South of France, writing the novel."

"The idea has faded from my mind."

She said, "My life will work out, I know. The security clearance is still valid, so I am eligible for odd work as a stringer. Sorties near the house in the Salzkammergut, courier duty across to Vienna. That could bring in a few hundred marks every now and then, enough for a round of blue cheese and a nice white wine."

Our group was dispersing, just as my time at Schloss Issel also came to a close. Callard and Captain McQuire were both reassigned duty at the CIC detachment in Beirut, a strange pair for the dark alleys of the Islam. Was the transfer more punishment than reward, Callard such an annoyance and McQuire's support of him an enigma to the higher ups? I was sure that Callard was already planning the perfect cut for a gallabiya, the correct wrapping of a head shawl and the shoes that would not give away an infidel agent. In his first week there he wrote a short card announcing his arrival and describing in detail the green lizard on the wall beside his cot, was he only gulping air or was he trying to say something important, a message from Bad Issel?

What the captain would do in the Lebanon was a mystery; she was like a water bird blown off her migration by unpleasant winds, a Kansas curiosity on the Levantine shore. However, I knew that she was resilient, able to make a place for herself, perhaps already enlisting a network of woman informants.

Parsons and Inga had left for Scranton, Pennsylvania, he on an airplane, she on a special ship for German brides. They looked so happy at their farewell party, that I had a wave of guilt over my skepticism, my dark thoughts about marriage proved wrong. For now, at least.

I was the last to leave, my final dossier still open on the desk, pens in a row beside it, as Callard had predicted, another young man sitting in my chair tomorrow. It was an early day in May quite different from the misty, dark evening of my arrival, the vines now in full leaf. It was a guardedly optimistic year for Bad Issel wine, everyone said, its pervasive sweetness on hold. The sun broke through fast moving clouds, but I had no temptation to look back at the Schloss as we drove away down the curving road.

# A Crescent of Easels

Being an old maid is like death by drowning,
a really delightful sensation after you cease to struggle.
— *Edna Ferber*

I HAD TWO HOURS BEFORE THE
next class, the eighteen sophomore students expecting to hear
from me the secrets to oil painting on a large canvas. It was
spring, the weather in Austin getting hotter as we approached
the end of the semester, the bluebells on the mall faded to
brown.

A swim in the apartment house pool would refresh me,
give me the stamina for a long studio class. It was ten minutes
later when I pulled the well-traveled Mercedes sedan, bud-vases
now empty, masterful engine still purring, into the parking
slot for Apartment 4-B. My cast-iron mail box on the walk was
bulging, so full that the mailman had not properly closed the
cover. Inside was a handful of envelopes, bills and mailers,
bound with a rubber band, courtesy US Post Office. I put the
packet into my canvas briefcase on the hall table and quickly
changed into swimming trunks. There was not enough time to

read mail and swim as well. I would open the day's letters when I got the students going on their paintings, after my thirty laps.

I said to the class, "Everybody pick the telling, perfect color and paint your plumb line on the canvas."

There were as many versions of a plumb line as there were students...the green one, thin and wobbly, fearfully dividing the canvas and a strong black one, almost exactly plumb, three inches wide itself, the canvas boldly underway, and an earth-red variation done in small angled strokes, top to bottom, like the petrified backbone of a long dead amphibian. The most promising student, Margaretta Dittrick had painted hers from bottom up to the top, confident and wide, leaving gaps of varying widths as she went up. Already her painting had rhythm and direction.

I liked teaching, but I wondered if painting could really be taught, or was it in the bones, like perfect pitch. Margaretta had it, whatever it was, and probably did not need a minute of my class. Drawing could be taught, but not painting itself. It was a heretical notion at a university art department, but I would continue teaching students to not quite paint. It gave me a way to be at the easel myself until I could paint every day on my own, make a life at art. Teaching was a stop-gap for me.

The plumb line was the literal spine of my method for teaching beginners to approach a large canvas, the idea handed to me so blithely by Miss Lender. The line violated the virginity of the white canvas, denying the terrible strength of its purity and giving the painter a hook to hang upon, a project with a beginning and an end. Divide and conquer. From here on, life would be getting better, as Miss Lender said. I read out the full quote from Matisse at the beginning of each semester, as well as other of his comments about the sense of verticality so vital to a canvas.

Margaretta was in love with me, a bad situation for an instructor, but nothing would ever come of it, despite her imprecations. I told her that I was a bachelor art professor and lived alone because I preferred the solitary life. There was no room for a young girl, however talented and promising she was.

She arranged her easel at the end of the large semi-circle, so others could not hear so well when I discussed her canvas. She tried everything to pique my interest, opening her blouse, sweetness, boldness, neediness, harshness, quietness, obscure quotes from art historians, questions about the Zen of a particular color, salacious offers and, several times, gushes of tears. I offered my kind, firm rejections, again and again. If obsession was all that guaranteed success in art, she would surely be the next O'Keeffe.

Through it all, she painted extraordinary canvases, one after the other, getting better and better. Following the exposed bosom business, she filled the panel with breasts and nipples of so many shapes that they mingled and merged into circles within circles, a mammary-invaded universe. After we talked about the correct color for passionate love, she mixed eighty shades of crimson and scarlet in small sharp cutting lines, as if a razor blade had slashed the painting, letting multi-colored bloods come through and dribble down. She could take in an event or idea in her own life and convert it into an exhilarating pattern, a matrix upon which she built the finished canvas. If we could complete our year together without open revolt, or mental breakdown on either side, she was well on her way into an art career. Her junior year, next year, other professors could then take the brunt of the attack, her laser love refocused on a new, unhappy target.

In the previous session, the entire class discussed the idea for this day's painting, a theme that all would attach to the plumb line, growing out from it, perhaps embellishing it, or replacing it. We considered unhappiness, madness, elation, childbirth and grief, but settled upon the motif of urbanity. They must put into paint what it was to be in the middle of a city today, equal parts of loneliness and joy. I would let them proceed on their own for the first hour, then make a slow progress across the crescent of easels, commenting, suggesting, questioning, sometimes actually demonstrating with paint on the student's canvas, finally at the end to a new confrontation with Margaretta. But, before that transit, while they started, I had time to look through my letters.

The top envelope was from the gallery in Santa Fe that handled my work. It reported that they had sold two paintings, check enclosed, please send some more with the same motif ASAP. This was the best sort of mail. Maybe my teaching days were coming to their end, no more needy Margarettas, the full-time painter Bradford bursting above the water line.

The next was from the Army National Guard, notifying me that my six-year service obligation had been completed, two years of active duty, followed by four of inactive. A handsome three-color Honorable Discharge certificate on card stock documenting this was already mailed under separate cover, signed by the Guard's commanding general.

My mother wrote of Dad's continued decline and, that spring had come to Middleton. The April Bird Census was a great success, despite the Steering Committee's grave questions over her solo sighting of a male Phainopepla, with his glossy blue-black feathers. Much too far from the seacoast.

There was an invitation to an art exhibit at a local Austin gallery, an electric bill, a gas bill, advertising flyers and one last envelope from Wisconsin. It was from Melanie Follum. I recognized her curvilinear script, wondering again if the flowing tracery resembled more the whip-lash or the spider web.

Melanie sent me regular letters on the details of their life together; how handsome Eric still was; how he had gained so little weight, unlike his brothers. She often talked about dinners she cooked for Eric; how they savored their time alone. But her real message was that if love was the Great War, the endless endeavor, she was the victor, and I was face-down in the sod. Eric was now hers, all hers. Her open friendliness suggested that the weapons were buried, bygones forgotten. I suspected that a true victor would not have to crow so loud and to walk so nervously along the frontiers.

They both worried, she often wrote, that I was still alone after all these years. I never received a letter from Eric himself, our parting night four years ago the last I touched him. I suspected his outgoing mail was closely monitored. I thought of Dumas's masked man deep in a French dungeon, straining to hear a sound through the thick masonry walls, a dear friend so close.

Eric and Melanie's marriage ceremony had been held in Wisconsin without me as the best man, during my semesters at art school. Every six or seven months a postcard arrived from their vacation destinations, mostly music-centered conventions around the world. Afterwards, Melanie sent snapshots of the happy couple. Both of them smiling on a bridge in Toronto, arm in arm on a palm-lined street in Los Angeles or in the midst of a bleacher filled with other organist couples. This was solid evidence that life was happy in the melodious northland.

This time the letter was three sentences in her florid script on the back of a printed card. She wrote:

> "We think of you so often, Eric and I, and wish you could be with us for Eric's conducting of the Spring Cantata,
> the full St. Olaf Philharmonic and the 100-voice university chorus.
> A secular cantata by J.S. Bach, you know.
> Love as always, Melanie."

The card was a printed invitation, yellow daisies in the corners, for a baptism at the Redeemer Lutheran Church of in late February, delivered three months late. The child's name was Mary Tangier Follum, our beloved daughter.

Melanie surely did not understand the real message in these

poignant remembrances, of a love not quite extinguished, thin curlicues of smoke hovering over the embers. Maybe on windy nights in the birch woods of Wisconsin there was a clandestine, pulsating red glow.

Now it was time to start my stroll along the crescent of easels, encouraging the work on this canvas, drawing a corrected line on that. *You must think of the canvas as whole, not an accidental meeting of pieces.* I lost focus at the fifth easel, gazing into a painting of solid blue, devoid of pattern, hypnotized while the student waited patiently for my commentary, my thoughts riding high above the ocean blue to an image fixed without change in my mind.

If a road divided in a wood, what must happen for the journey back in time on a small Tabriz, flying high over the earthly hours, undoing the hills and valleys between here and the past, erasing the days and nights, undulating backwards over clusters of reasonable people, people who said they loved you, people who asked for obligations, to land again at that forested convergence and walk the other way, the route that looked so impossible back then, so unrewarding?

www.ingramcontent.com/pod-product-compliance
Lightning Source LLC
Chambersburg PA
CBHW011356010726
47494CB00008B/2337